MALICE

THE TENTH PETE CULNANE MYSTERY

S.L. Smith

St. Paul, Minnesota

ISBN: 979-8-9868405-2-9

Second Edition, August 2025

Printed in the United States of America

Cover designed by Christopher Smith

SIGHTLINE PRESS
St. Paul, Minnesota 55117
www.slsmithbooks.com

For all my nieces and nephews, and great nieces and
nephews. In your own special way, each of you has
added so much to my life. Thanks.

.

ONE
Unanticipated Exit

At 5:10 a.m. Fred Brooten uttered a string of expletives as he tugged on his down jacket and zipped it up to his chin. Then he pulled his stocking cap down until it covered his ears and was so close to his eyes that it jeopardized his ability to see. He'd listened to the news and weather while getting ready for work. After two weeks of what appeared to be an early spring, St. Paul was back in the deep freeze. Sure, the temperature was 20 degrees, but with northerly winds of 20 and gusting to 40 mph, the windchill was below zero.

"It's April, for crying out loud," he muttered, "and I just got accustomed to manageable temperatures." Yanking on his warmest gloves, he stormed out the door of his condo with little regard for the loud slam behind him.

Oh yeah, he thought as he rushed to the stairway, *I need to add the elimination of that obnoxious racket to my list of improvements for this place.* Fred considered himself to be the sole reason that property values of the condos in this complex hadn't plummeted.

When he bought his unit four years ago, it was a "real steal." He believed that was because the board of directors had let things slide. Seeing the possibilities and determined to change things, he ran for a slot on the board of directors for the annual meeting scheduled to be held two years ago. As was apparently often the case for this association, the board didn't have a quorum, so the annual meeting couldn't be held.

Not to be deterred, Fred kissed up to several board members and busted his butt until they were compelled to appoint him to fill a vacancy while waiting for the next annual meeting. He figured he'd be indispensable by then and an obvious shoo-in.

That was two years ago, and Fred was still on the board by virtue of that appointment. He surmised that the majority of the owners obviously didn't care what was done in and around the complex, and he took advantage of their apathy.

Just a few months after his appointment, he'd fast-talked and worked hard enough to sell the other members of the board on naming him their president. Since then, he achieved his priorities with few if any constraints.

When talking to the board and the residents, he referred to those projects as "maintenance." Otherwise, per the governing documents, he had to get member approval before spending as little as a thousand dollars on any single project. If he waited for an annual meeting and the approval of a majority of the members before proceeding, nothing would ever happen. Fred grinned with satisfaction when he thought about the numerous times he'd gotten around that stupid stumbling-block.

But his smile quickly transitioned to a frown. Based on the number of complaints submitted to the management company over the last few months, things might soon become much more difficult.

Fred was furious that so many owners permitted the necessary increases in their monthly dues to dictate their opinions. *Why can't they understand the benefits of what I'm doing? Why can't they see beyond their collective noses? This is a volunteer position! Talk about a bunch of ingrates! No wonder they have so much trouble filling vacancies on the board.*

Fred clomped down the stairs, oblivious to the racket created by his six foot two, 260 pounds. At least that was what his driver's license said he weighed. In the process, he awakened the residents with bedrooms bordering this stairway who'd somehow slept through his slamming door. Right now, all he cared about was the weather and having to go outside to reach his car and struggle to start it in this sub-zero temperature.

Most of his neighbors didn't have to go outside to reach their vehicles, and the fact he did was of his own making, though not really his fault. He had to find a place to store the stuff that had filled his four-bedroom home and wouldn't fit in this two-bedroom condo. He wasn't about to pay a storage fee, so he'd jammed the stuff into his garage. It was the only option—aside from working some sort of deal with the witch to whom he'd been married for a decade and a half. The garage was so packed, he'd have been hard-pressed to find enough room for something as small as a college yearbook.

Having failed to sort through and get rid of all that stuff, which his ex called "crap," he was forced to park in one of the too-few spots in the parking lot. After all, it wasn't his fault that whipping this condominium complex into shape, while ensuring it was safe and had curb appeal, took so much time. Add to that, he had to keep his kids in line and on track academically, and make sure the people who worked for him toed the line. All of that left little time for anything else. It angered him that none of them appreciated all he did to make their lives better. His lack of availability had even cost him many of his friends, but he couldn't worry about that. At least for now, there were too many other, more important things on his agenda. He truly loved the power and prestige that being the president of the condo association provided.

Fred ran all out to his truck, using a pace that most guys his age would have defined as a jog. As he scraped the ice off his windshield and windows, he swore he'd get rid of all of the things in his garage that forced him to park outside on days like this.

Unbeknownst to him, that would never happen. Time had run out for Fred. The stuff in his garage was about to become someone else's problem.

Two

He's Back

Again this morning, Pete rocked Teddy to sleep after his morning feeding. He was immersed in the joys of fatherhood, singing to him about buying him a mocking bird. This was day four since his paternity leave ended, and he'd been able to do this each morning. But he wasn't holding his breath about it becoming a habit. Things were certain to change. The only question was when the call would come, and he'd once again be wrapped up in a case and bent on solving it ASAP. He refused to permit that looming reality to diminish the happiness that times like this provided. He'd waited a long time for this to happen.

Once Teddy drifted off to sleep, Pete smiled and stood, kissed his son's forehead, and gently laid him in his crib. Then as he straightened up, and Benji, their puppy, arranged himself on the floor in front of the crib, Pete heard it. The ring tone on his cellphone announced the call was work-related.

Katie jumped when she heard the ringing, then sighed, knowing what it had to mean. Realizing with the cessation of Pete's singing that Teddy must be asleep, she smiled. At least their treasured moment hadn't been interrupted this morning.

She loved having Pete home for Teddy's morning nursing and for dinner, being able to discuss her day and his, and crawling into bed together at night. If that call meant what she thought it did, those things were about to come to a screeching halt for at least several days.

Katie didn't begrudge this interruption by a job that brought Pete so much satisfaction and fulfillment. He'd been back on the job for less than a week and hadn't yet decided whether to remain a detective with the St. Paul Police Department.

Grabbing Pete's cell, she hurried to the nursery, and Pete intercepted her just outside the room. He wore a combination of a smile and a look of resignation as she handed him the phone.

"Culnane," he answered, then listened intently.

The caller was Commander Lincoln, the St. Paul PD head of the Homicide and Robbery Unit. He was assigning Pete to investigate a shooting on Jackson Street just north of the intersection with Maryland Avenue. He said the Forensic Services Unit was already on the way, and he was calling Martin next.

The team is back, Pete thought and smiled.

Hurrying to their bedroom with Katie on his heels, he shared the scarce details.

Pete was glad he'd showered and shaved while Katie nursed Teddy, so all he had to do was dress and head out. He figured he'd reach the crime scene well ahead of Martin, since Martin was only out of bed this early if he'd scheduled something for the two of them.

Katie checked the road conditions and the weather as he dressed, then followed him through the kitchen to the back door.

After putting on his overcoat and grabbing his gloves, he stopped long enough to kiss her good-bye. Then he reached for the doorknob.

Katie tapped him on the shoulder and held out his stocking cap. "Windchills are in the teens below zero; you'll need this." She smiled.

Pete grinned, took it, gave her a peck on the cheek, and was off.

He thought about calling Martin, but decided against it, not wanting to slow Martin down.

As Katie noted, the roads were dry, thanks to the warmup they'd enjoyed during the final days of March. Aside from a few obstinate mounds in spaces like parking lots, the snow was gone—at least for now. Heaven only knew what April and May would bring. The lack of snow might be unfortunate when it came to this case, since snow, especially a new coating, could provide valuable leads.

After considering the options, Pete decided to follow Wheelock Parkway to Jackson Street and take Jackson south to the crime scene.

On the way, he thought about the case. *Why was the victim out this early in the morning? Was it the norm? How long had the victim lain there before being discovered? There wasn't much traffic on Jackson at this hour. Did anyone witness the attack? If so, would they come forward?*

He pictured the intersection of Jackson with Maryland. There were stoplights there. Maryland was four lanes at that point, and Jackson was two. A compact parking lot for the Troutbrook Nature Sanctuary, where he often parked to go running, was located on the northeast corner of the intersection. A couple of businesses that would be uninhabited at this hour stood on the west side. On the south side, he knew the intersection on both the east and west sides of Jackson was a good half block from the closest homes. Pete considered, *Was the relative seclusion the reason the crime happened here? If so, it had to be premeditated, and why this morning? Why didn't the shooter wait for a warmer morning? What drove the act and the timing?*

As anticipated, he encountered a roadblock at Arlington, the last street crossing Jackson before Maryland. Pete identified himself to a uniformed officer staffing the barrier, then drove around it. Approaching Maryland, he saw the FSU crime scene response vehicle parked along Jackson just north of Maryland.

After pulling over his unmarked car and parking behind several squads and the Ramsey County ME van also stopped along Jackson, Pete opened the door and was greeted by a wind gust that pushed him up against the door. Thanking Katie for her watchfulness, he reached in, grabbed his stocking cap, and pulled it down over his ears.

He'd just bested the wind by getting the car door closed when he felt his cellphone vibrate in his trouser pocket. Pulling off a glove, he extracted it and glanced at the screen. Choosing comfort and sanity over a demonstration of his endurance, Pete got back in the car, closed the door, pulled off his stocking cap, and answered.

Pete figured Martin was calling to advise him of his ETA.

"Where are you?" Martin asked.

"Jackson and Maryland."

"Thought I'd beat you this once," Martin said and groaned. "I'm just getting on I-35E. See you in a few," and he disconnected.

Braving the elements, Pete again pulled his stocking cap down low and exited his car. Stepping far enough out on Jackson to see around the FSU vehicle, he caught sight of the lead investigator with the Ramsey County Medical Examiner's office. Don was one of three people bundled up and crouched over a body lying on Jackson, near the entrance to the Troutbrook Nature Sanctuary parking lot and across the street from a red GMC Sierra 1500. With so many flood lights, courtesy of the FSU, all the details were clearly visible even though the sun wouldn't rise for almost an hour.

With no further delay, Pete approached an investigator with the FSU, digging for additional details.

THREE

The Crime Scene

"Thanks to this weather, are you cursing the shooter's selection of this date and time, Jeff?" Pete smiled at the FSU investigator controlling the crime scene.

"Damn straight! Couldn't this have waited until the temperature approached zero and the winds weren't so strong that it's hard to stand still? Right now, an extra fifty pounds would come in mighty handy." Jeff's ski mask hid his own smile, but his voice left no doubt of its presence.

"Reported via 911?" Pete asked.

"Yup. The call came in at 5:31. Caller stayed put until we arrived, but has since departed. Got her contact information. She had to get moving. Scheduled for surgery at Regions. She's the doctor, not the patient. Told her you'd need to speak with her, and she said you could reach her between 11:00 and 1:30 or after 4:30. You can find her at Regions. Nice woman."

"Name?"

"Dr. Ruth Kinney." Jeff pulled her business card out of a jacket pocket and handed it to Pete. "Reported that, as she drove up, someone got into a car in the oncoming lane across from that GMC and drove away," Jeff said, nodding at the Sierra. "Said she doesn't know if it was a man or a woman. Heck, it's almost impossible to tell with the way most people dress in these temperatures. She couldn't identify the make or model of the vehicle, but said it was mid-sized and white. Anyway, she got out of her car and checked for a pulse. After failing to find one, she returned to her car and called 911."

Pete nodded and asked, "Did she think the person who took off was the shooter?"

Jeff's answer was drowned out by a train approaching down the hill just east of them. Neither Jeff's face mask nor Pete's stocking cap helped with that.

Pete took a step closer, into Jeff's personal space and said, "Come again?"

"She had no idea," Jeff hollered.

"What do you have so far?" Pete asked, volume raised, since the train made hearing impossible any other way. That continued for nearly five minutes, until the train was gone.

Martin arrived in time to hear Jeff say, "According to the driver's license in his wallet, the victim's name is Frederick Brooten, and he lived in an apartment just off Larpenteur, between Rice Street and Dale. We also found a badge that indicates he worked for Fundamentals Insurance."

"Someone took at least two shots at Brooten's front, driver's-side tire," Jeff continued. "The shooter made short work of that tire, hitting the tread twice. They may have aimed for the tread, since for an oncoming vehicle it's a larger and more stationary target than the sidewall."

Glancing from Pete to Martin, he added, "It also means the shooter was positioned ahead of Brooten as he approached Maryland. Based on the marks the bullet left on the wheel, we've also determined the shooter was a bit right of Brooten's approaching truck."

Looking back at the tire, he said, "The condition of the tire appears to have caused Brooten to stop almost immediately, and the condition of the rim supports that conclusion."

Pete spoke loudly to be heard, "If someone shot out one of my tires, I wouldn't stop. I'd drive on the rim until I was clear of the area, and then some."

Martin nodded.

Jeff chuckled and said, "But the two of you are paranoid. What if this guy had no idea someone might be after him? Check out that tire. It would make for mighty tough going."

"Unless his radio was blaring, the sound of the gunshots should have provided a pretty clear warning that he had a reason to be afraid," Pete shouted.

"Only if the shooter didn't use a silencer," Jeff answered. "And if there was a train passing at the time the shots were fired, as is currently being demonstrated, Pete, the racket made by the train could have masked the sound of the shots. I checked. Trains pass through here with monotonous regularity, and there is one scheduled at 5:20 a.m. Monday through Friday."

"If the shooter was depending on that train for camouflage," Pete said, "they were a total optimist, a gambler, extremely lucky, and/or well versed in the train and Brooten's scheduled and actual arrivals."

Jeff shrugged and continued, "We're wondering why he crossed Jackson." He nodded at the body. "Did he see the person who shot out his tire? Was he chasing them? Is that why he was shot? If he believed he saw that person, he must have known they had a gun. Why wouldn't he run the other way? I guess determining all of those things is your job, huh?

"The position of the body makes it look like he was diving into a swimming pool," Jeff continued. "His head was up, and his arms and hands were stretched straight out from his shoulders. It looks like he was lunging at someone or something when he was shot.

"So far," he added, "we've found one 9 mm cartridge on the road between the top of his head and the curb, and two more by that thick patch of underbrush." Jeff pointed at the area alongside Jackson and on the northwestern edge of the Troutbrook parking lot. "The ones near the undergrowth could mean the shooter waited there for Brooten's truck to come over the hill and approach Maryland. That would be consistent with the angle at which the bullets hit the tire. Needless to say, we're scouring Jackson, in the vicinity of his truck and his body, the Troutbrook Sanctuary, parking lot, and environs."

The racket from the train dissipated as Pete and Martin thanked Jeff and greeted several FSU investigators who were scouring and photographing the scene as they walked over to Don and the victim.

"Congratulations on the baby," Don said. "We've missed you. The person targeting this guy wasn't leaving anything to chance. Based on the locations of the casing, they were almost in his face when they shot him in the neck. As you can see, the body is stretched out in a curious position, so it appears he died instantly—before he could react to being shot. We'll know a lot more after the autopsy. Getting ready to load the body and take him downtown. Should know the time for the autopsy by midafternoon."

Walking to their unmarked cars, Martin told Pete, "The sanctuary parking lot doesn't open until sunrise, so how about if we drop your car off at headquarters and I'll drive to our next location?"

Pete looked to the east and saw the sky beginning to lighten along the horizon. It was still half an hour until sunrise, but the pinks and yellows added some color to the black, overcast sky. "First, let's notify the victim's family. Headquarters is in the opposite direction from his home address. So follow me. I'll find a place on the way to ditch my car and ride the rest of the way with you."

Martin liked that idea, so they did.

After parking, while sliding into Martin's car, Pete smiled and thought, *Picking up where we left off.*

FOUR
The Victim's Home

Ten minutes later, thanks to the lack of traffic and Martin's failure to respect the speed limits, they arrived at the address on Brooten's driver's license. The complex consisted of eight buildings arranged in an irregular oval, interspersed with patches of dead grass, and surrounding a parking lot. Frederick Brooten's building was at the far end of the layout. The buildings in the complex appeared well maintained, and there was no evidence of extravagance or extra amenities.

Nearly melted mounds of snow lingered along the perimeter of the parking lot and appeared blue in the predawn light. Parking spots were at a premium, so Martin had to park half a lot away from Brooten's building. For that reason, he wore his stocking cap when they left the car. Pete didn't, deciding he wouldn't be outside very long. Besides, his thick hair provided significant insulation.

Wind chills hadn't improved noticeably, so the two investigators jogged from the car to Brooten's entrance. Due to Pete's long legs, this required less effort for him.

Based on the lack of illuminated windows, very few of the residents in this complex were stirring.

The doorbells were located on an exterior panel, so visitors had to wait outside until given access to these secure buildings. A narrow overhang provided minimal protection for anyone awaiting a response to the doorbells. Removing his right glove, Martin pressed Brooten's doorbell.

Nothing happened.

He waited impatiently for a minute at most, then tried again.

When the result was the same, Pete rang the doorbell of the apartment one number higher than Brooten's. Although he had no way of knowing the layout, based on the arrangement of the doorbells, he thought it was likely one of the apartments with lights turned on.

He smiled when a voice announced, "Whatever you're selling, I don't want any! What are you doing bothering people this early in the morning, and didn't you see the sign that says no soliciting?"

"Police," he said. "We're trying to reach Frederick Brooten's family, and no one answers. Does he live alone?"

"Yes, and I don't know if he has any family."

"Is there a manager?"

"There's a management company, but no one will be in at this hour."

"Can you please give us their phone number and address?"

"Yes, and I'll let you in. Based on the radio reports, it's too cold to stand out there while I find the information." She had little more than said that when there was a buzz and a click.

Martin grabbed the doorknob and opened the door, not risking it relocking before they got inside. He'd been down this road before.

Little more than a minute later, an elderly woman with wispy gray hair and a deeply lined face came barreling down the stairs at a pace that would be noteworthy for someone a decade or two younger.

"She's in mighty good shape for someone her age," Martin said softly, out of the corner of his mouth.

The woman introduced herself as Kathy Wheaton and handed Martin a piece of paper. "I wrote it all down for you. Is there a problem?"

"We're pressed for time right now," Martin said, "but might want to speak with you later."

Kathy shrugged, rattled off her phone number so fast Pete had to ask her to repeat it, then she headed back up the stairs as rapidly as she'd come down. It reminded Pete of Grandma Jackie, his mom's mom.

Before they exited the building, Martin called the number Kathy gave him.

As she predicted, he got a voicemail message, saying the hours were 9:00 until 4:00, Monday through Friday. Then it gave the emergency number. As soon as the automated voice began reciting that number, he told Pete, "Help me remember this number," and he repeated it as it was recited.

Pete grabbed his phone out of his pocket and entered the digits. The recording repeated the number, Martin did likewise, and Pete double-checked the number on his screen. Then he pressed the call button.

The calls were answered by a service that determined which calls qualified as emergencies. When Pete said he was a police officer, he made the cut, and he was given the phone number for the owner or representative of the management company.

A sleepy voice answered on the seventh ring, and Pete explained he was a police officer and needed

Frederick Brooten's emergency contact. He didn't even know if the management company had emergency contacts for the residents, but it only seemed reasonable.

The sleepy voice said all of that information was at his office, and he'd get back to Pete at 9:00 a.m.

Pete explained there were two ways they could do this. Either the guy on the other end of the line could get him the emergency contact's name, address, and phone number in the next several minutes, or the police would get a search warrant and find it themselves.

"But ..."

"Thirty minutes or else."

Pete and Martin had done little more than reach Martin's unmarked car and buckled in when Pete's phone vibrated. It was the last number he'd called.

Pete pulled out his notepad and a pen, answered, and put the call on speaker.

"This is George from Eagle Management. I got the information you requested. Fred's emergency contact is Julie Brooten. She's his ex-wife. I'm surprised he still has her listed. Things are not good between them," George said, and recited her address and phone number.

Not taking any chances, Pete repeated the address and phone number, and George verified both.

As soon as Pete had done so, George said, "What happened to Fred?"

Without waiting for an answer, he added, "I hope he'll be fine. He's a real asset to his condominium association. Little would be accomplished without him, and he stays on top of things. Thanks to him, a lot of changes and improvements have occurred: The place would fall apart without him."

"By the way," Pete said, "I also need the names, addresses, and phone numbers for the other members of the board of directors."

"What did you say happened to Fred?"

"I didn't, and how about the information I requested, regarding the other members of the board?"

"I don't think you should bother them. We tell the owners to come to me and not bother the board if they have issues."

"I'm not an owner. What are their names, addresses, and phone numbers?"

Grudgingly, George recited and Pete wrote down that information for the vice president, secretary, treasurer, and the member-at-large.

George ended by saying, "You know, that association has a lot of critical items pending. I'm going to have to scramble if Fred's unable to continue as the president, so I think you should give me a heads-up on what is happening, and the outlook."

"I'll be sure you have all the information you should have when you should have it. Thanks for your help, George."

Pete disconnected and rolled his eyes. Then he called the first of Julie Brooten's two phone numbers. George didn't know if it was her work, home phone, or cell number.

It was a few minutes before 7:00, and Julie Brooten answered. "Judith, is that you? No one else calls this early."

Appears this phone doesn't have caller ID, Pete thought and smiled. Otherwise, likely as not, people ignored a call when instead of a phone number the screen read "Blocked."

He identified himself and explained he needed to meet with her right away. "My partner and I will be there in twenty minutes," he said.

"Regarding?" she asked.

"See you shortly," Pete said, verified the address George provided, and disconnected.

FIVE
Victim's Ex-wife

Julie Brooten lived in a middle-class neighborhood, circa the 1960s and 1970s, in Inver Grove Heights, a Dakota County suburb south of St. Paul. Aside from its cream color, there was little to distinguish her split-level from those up and down her street.

Pete figured she'd been watching for them, because she opened the front door and stood behind the storm door as they walked up her driveway.

She appeared to be in her mid- to late-fifties, was tall, attractive, and athletic looking. She had shoulder-length dishwater-blonde hair and stern blue eyes that looked wary.

As they reached her, without opening the door, she asked, "What's this all about?"

"It's pretty cold out here," Pete said. "You might save on your heating bill by inviting us in, rather than talking through a storm door."

"First, prove you're police officers."

As soon as both men extracted and displayed their badges and IDs, Julie opened the storm door and stepped aside. The moment they were inside, she repeated her question.

"I'm sorry to have to tell you that Frederick was attacked early this morning and died," Pete said.

Julie slumped back against the wall and, nervously running her fingers through her hair, asked, "What? He's dead? He's actually dead?" She looked from Pete to Martin, and they both nodded.

Looking horrified she blurted out, "What am I going to do without the child support? I'm barely able to make the mortgage payments with it, and I have no idea how I'll manage without that money. I believe he lied about his income, and the payments were far below what they should have been, but at least I managed. Now I'll have to get a second and maybe even a third job," she sighed, "and that will be unfair to the kids, especially my youngest, Sam. Let's go sit down. I feel like I've just had the wind knocked out of me."

Pushing herself away from the wall, she led them to the family room. On the way, with her back to them, she said, "How did it happen?"

Before Pete or Martin could reply, she added, "Just so you know, were it not for the child support, I'd be glad he's gone. And three of our four kids feel the same way."

The two investigators waited until they were seated in an economically but tastefully decorated room and facing her to respond. Then Pete said, "He may have been on his way to work when he was attacked."

"You said it happened early this morning. Early like around 5:00?"

Pete nodded.

"For years he insisted on getting to work by 5:30. That's more than an hour before anyone else. If there was a good reason, he refused to share it. I really needed his help with the kids in the morning, but that's neither here nor there. What happened to him? Was he alone? He was so afraid of dying alone."

That sounds more like an observation than a concern, Pete thought. Because she was a suspect, he said, "At the present time, we're not able to share any details. Where did he work?"

"At Fundamentals Insurance Company."

"How long has he worked there?" Pete asked.

"At least twenty years. He started working there shortly after our first child was born."

To develop a broader picture of Brooten, Pete began a series of questions, starting with, "How long were you married?"

"Fifteen years, eight months, two days, seven hours and ..." looking at her watch she added, "thirty-seven minutes, even though I discovered the real Fred within a week of our wedding and should have been smart enough to leave him then." She grimaced. "It was a marriage from hell, and the only good thing to come out of it was our four children." Julie's head dropped and she resumed running her fingers through her hair.

"What changed?"

"Fred from A to Z. He became my jailer and my master. I couldn't go anywhere or do anything without his permission. He told me how to dress and how to raise our children, and he blew up if I didn't do both exactly as he'd instructed. I had a job working nights, which I loved; and he forced me to quit it, so I was accessible to him whenever the spirit moved him. He was always right and, whenever anything went wrong, it was someone else's fault. I could go on and on, but I'm sure you've got the picture." Julie shook her head forlornly.

"How long have you been divorced?"

"Going on six years."

Taking a turn, Martin began by asking, "How many children do you and Fred have, and how old are they?"

"Adam is twenty-one, Paul is eighteen, Emily is sixteen, and Sam is fourteen. In case you didn't notice, in order of oldest to youngest, their initials spell APES. I didn't realize that until Sam was baptized and Fred told me. He'd been planning it ever since Adam was born. I should have known. It wasn't like I didn't know him by then. He picked all four names and wouldn't budge an inch when I suggested other names. Names I was fond of, such as the names of family members who had passed. After Sam was baptized, he never called any of the kids by their names. Instead, they were Ape One, Ape Two, etcetera. He thought it was hilarious and so clever. For an adolescent, perhaps. NOT for a grown man. Only Sam thought it was funny, but he IS an adolescent, and he's definitely his father's son."

Frowning, she continued, "Still can't believe I was stupid enough to fall for Fred, but he put on a good act while we were dating. Some couples grow apart. That happened on our honeymoon, but I spent more than fifteen years trying to make things work. Threw in the towel when he added physical abuse to the psychological and verbal abuse." Julie sat back in her chair, relaxed a few degrees, but kept wringing her hands.

"When did the physical abuse begin?" Pete asked.

"About a year before the divorce was finalized. The first time he hit me, I told myself it was an exception and wouldn't happen again. I might have been able to rationalize the second attack a few weeks later, had he not also slapped poor little Emily. She was a petite nine-year-old, and he slapped her so hard he left a red blotch on her cheek. She cowered in a corner and cried. I knew

I could never let that happen again. Cracking my ribs and bruising my torso and buttocks was one thing. Attacking one of the children was a whole different story. That's when I knew I had to stop him. So I called the police, threw him out, and got a restraining order. By doing those things, I knew, given the chance, his physical attacks on me would escalate, but I did it anyway. I didn't think I had a choice, and I believe that to this day. Fortunately, since then, he hasn't had a chance to lay a hand on me, and I am so very grateful for that. Given the chance, I think he'd have found a cold and calculating way to kill me. I'm sure he wanted to."

"He wanted to, but didn't find a way to make it happen?"

"He'd have had to make it look like an accident. I'd be surprised if he didn't spend hours trying to find a way. Maybe the opportunity hadn't yet happened. I spent a lot of time watching over my shoulder for him."

"Did he lose all parental rights?"

"No, but I told him if he wanted to see the kids, he had to call, arrange something, and meet them somewhere. He couldn't be alone with them, and he couldn't come here."

"Did he do those things?" Martin asked.

"Rarely. I don't even know when he last saw them, but they could have been meeting with him when I was at work."

"Do all four of your children live here with you?" Martin asked.

"Regrettably, no. Adam was never a student. After he graduated from high school, he got a job and moved out. Fred was always on his back and calling him a loser for not going to college. Paul graduates this spring and is scheduled to start at Metro State University in the fall.

He's already earned I don't even know how many college credits. He, Emily, and Sam still live here with me. None of them, not even Sam, wanted to move in with their father. Glad I didn't have to fight to protect them from him."

"Where does Adam work?" Martin asked.

"Regions Hospital. He's a maintenance engineer. Adam's no slacker, and they love him. He lives with several buddies and is a saver. But he gives me money every few months to help me make ends meet."

"Where do Paul, Emily, and Sam go to school?" Martin asked.

Julie recited the names of the high school Paul and Emily attended as well as Sam's middle school, and Pete made notes in the notepad he was never without.

"Sam gets home around 3:30," she continued, "and I'd have to check Emily and Paul's schedules. They have so many activities and clubs."

Martin didn't tell her they needed that information, because they'd be the ones breaking the news to her kids, while determining whether any of them played a part in their father's death. For the time being, she was still a suspect, having openly disclosed a motive. They still had to determine whether she'd be permitted to be present when they spoke with her kids.

"What shift does Adam work?" Martin asked. *And what I really want to know is whether he could have been at Jackson and Maryland around 5:00 this morning,* Martin thought but didn't share.

"Last I heard, 7:00 until 3:00, but I doubt he'd be willing to meet with you during his work hours."

"I assume he has a cell," Pete said.

Julie nodded.

When he asked for the number, she left them long enough to retrieve her cell, then recited the number, while Pete jotted it down in his notepad. Then he said, "He probably doesn't want to be called while working, huh?"

"No, for sure. I don't think his supervisor would like it."

Having helped Julie come to that conclusion and counting on her to stick with it, he said, "I know school buses pick some kids up mighty early these days. What time do your kids get up for school?"

"Sam is up and rolling by 6:30. He has to be out the door by 6:55, but has getting ready down to a science and eats breakfast on his way out the door." Julie smiled for the first time. "Paul and Emily get up at 6:45. Wish I could afford to get them a car, so they could get more sleep. It infuriates me that Fred bought a GMC Sierra for something like $80,000, yet couldn't manage to keep up with his child support payments. One good thing, or what could have been a good thing, happened thanks to that purchase. I found out he got a significant bump in pay. Scheduled a court date to get an increase in his child support payments. Now that will never happen, and the child support just dried up." Julie sighed deeply and shook her head.

"There's a good chance his employer carries life insurance on its employees," Martin said. "That might provide significant assistance."

"If there is a life insurance policy, he probably didn't name me as the beneficiary."

"You were listed as his emergency contact at the condominium complex where he lived," Martin said. "That's how we got your address and phone number. Who else would he designate?"

"He moved into a condo?" Julie asked wide-eyed.

Martin nodded.

"Going back to your problems with his child support payments," Pete said, "didn't Child Support Services have his wages garnished, so you didn't have to worry about regular payments for the correct amount?"

While clenching and unclenching her fists, Julie said, "Fred told me I would regret getting them involved. I don't know what he could have done, but I was afraid he'd find a way to make that happen. Also, every penny was and still is important. So I didn't want to have to pay a monthly fee for their services. And even if they were involved, knowing Fred, I don't believe he'd have accurately reported his income. I'm sure his bonuses and all similar earnings would have slipped through the cracks."

"Are his parents alive?" Pete asked.

"His mother died when he was ten. According to Fred, she got cancer and refused treatment. He hated her for that, even though he knew nothing about her reasons. There have been times when I wondered if it was a way to escape Fred's dad. His dad died last summer. Fred was a chip off the old block. His dad was an angry, demanding, know-it-all."

"Did he have any brothers or sisters?" Martin asked.

"He had two brothers. Steve died a couple of years ago in a car accident. He was a good man and always in my corner. I dated him for a short time before I began dating Fred. Can't tell you how many times I've wished I'd married Steve. I honestly don't understand how he and Fred could be brothers. The same is true for his brother Pat. He's a great guy who also sided with me whenever he heard Fred cutting me to ribbons. They had the same parents and grew up in the same environment.

How could they be so radically different? My sister insisted Fred was possessed."

"What's your sister's name?" Pete asked.

"Judith. She and her family live in North Carolina. Her husband is career military and is assigned to Fort Bragg. I haven't seen her in years, but she calls regularly. I can't afford to go there, but hope she'll soon find a way to come home for a visit. She has two-year-old twins, so the thought of traveling with them is pretty overwhelming."

"What's Judith's last name?" Pete asked.

"Winton."

"Does she know about the magnitude of your problems with Fred?" Pete asked.

"Well, yes. She and I talk about him almost every time we speak. She told me that the kids and I should move to Fayetteville so she and her husband could provide more assistance. I told her there was no way I could manage that."

"Any friends you were able to talk to?" Martin asked.

"After I married Fred, my friends drifted away, one by one. They wanted nothing to do with him, and I was tied up most of the time with him and the kids, so our connections slowly evaporated."

"Do you have any brothers?" Martin asked.

"No, I sure could have used at least one to defend me against Fred." Julie moaned.

"Did Fred's brother Pat know how bad things got with you and Fred?" Martin asked.

"If you mean did he know Fred was behind on child support, yes. Other than that, I don't think so. I was hesitant to share my fears with him. It didn't seem fair to do what seemed like pitting them against one another."

"Tell us about your brother-in-law Pat," Pete said.

"He has a consulting company. His office is in downtown St. Paul. He's the one who told me about Fred's new truck. Pat loves the kids, helps them with school activity fees, and is always buying them stuff. He also regularly takes them out to dinner or brings takeout when I'm working." Julie smiled again.

"Where does he live?" Martin asked.

"Eagan. He never married, but seems content."

Pete made a note of Pat's phone numbers, and work and home addresses, then asked if Fred had any sisters.

"None. Do you suppose the problem was that he never learned how to treat a woman?"

"Did he treat men any better?" Martin asked.

"Good point, but I think he might have been less confident of his ability to control other men. It's hard knowing. I tried to get him to go with me to a marriage counselor. He wanted nothing to do with it." Julie frowned.

"How about your parents?" Martin asked. "Do they provide any emotional or financial support?"

"I didn't know until I began sharing my problems with them that neither Mom nor Dad liked Fred. You see, based on the experiences of their friends, they'd learned the fastest way to get a daughter to marry someone was to criticize him or advise against it. They did encourage me to take my time, and later I wondered if Fred knew it was because they didn't like him. He insisted we marry less than six months after we started dating because, he said, he couldn't get more than an occasional day off here and there for another year. I shouldn't have permitted that to convince me and, of course, I paid dearly for buying that line." Julie sighed and shook her head miserably.

"Mom and Dad moved to Arizona shortly after Dad retired and right before I got married. Mom flew up for a week and helped each time I had a new baby. That gave her a wonderful opportunity to bond with my kids. Fred was off with his dad much of that time. That should have been a good indication of what lay ahead, shouldn't it?" Julie sighed and shook her head.

"Getting back to your question, money is tight for them, but they frequently offer financial assistance. I only accept when I'm in a real bind. On the other hand, they are quick to lend an ear, and they are excellent sounding blocks. We talk every Sunday afternoon."

"What's happened in the last few months to make you more afraid of your ex-husband?" Martin asked.

Julie sat awhile, staring into space, then said, "Nothing. I've been scared to death of him for at least six years."

"In that case, what's happened to make you or your kids hate him more?" Martin asked.

"The fact he bought a new car. We're struggling, and he buys a flashy new truck? Give me a break." She frowned.

"Where do you work?" Pete asked.

"At a restaurant in downtown St. Paul. They are trying to help me survive financially, so they allow me to work the lunch rush, then come home to be here when Sam gets home, and return for the dinner rush. The tips are better than good, and I think some of the regulars are also trying to help. Don't know what I'd do without that job."

"What time do you get home from each shift?" Pete asked.

"I get here about 2:30 and return to work about 3:45. And I get home at the end of the day between 8:30 and 9:00."

"You said Adam has a cell," Pete said. "How about Paul, Emily, and Sam?"

"They've bugged me like crazy to get them phones. Most of their friends have them. There's no way I can swing that."

"Does Paul or Emily have a job?" Martin asked.

"Yes, Paul's primary job is to keep his grades up and research scholarship possibilities, and he does yardwork for some of the neighbors for spending money. Emily's primary job is riding herd on Sam while I'm working, and she also babysits."

"Based on what you've told us, you were afraid of Fred," Pete said.

"Of course I was."

"What steps did you take to protect yourself, aside from getting a restraining order?" Pete asked.

"Like what? Hire a bodyguard?" she said sarcastically.

Pete and Martin said nothing.

Finally, after the silence grew uncomfortable, she added, "Changed all the locks for more secure ones and installed a security system. I keep, I mean kept, an eye out for him whenever I was out. What else could I do?"

"These days, the purchase of a firearm is pretty common," Pete said.

Julie gazed at him blankly.

"You don't have any firearms?" Pete asked.

Julie sat silently for a while, staring at her lap, then said, "I know it would have been a good idea, but I had no idea how to go about getting a gun. It's all pretty complex, isn't it?"

"Have you ever fired a gun?" Martin asked.

"No. I have no idea how to handle one, put the bullets in, aim, or fire it. I'd be scared to death to shoot one."

"Are you handing us a line?" Pete asked, looking her straight in the eye.

Julie looked past him and shook her head.

Neither Pete nor Martin was convinced she didn't have a firearm. She was far more convincing about never having fired one. At least for now, they wouldn't attempt to try to talk her into searching her house. They didn't have a search warrant, and thus far they had no grounds for getting one. So they dropped the subject, hoping they hadn't already convinced her to dispose of it—if she had one.

They thanked her for her assistance and left.

After watching them stride down her driveway, Julie returned to the family room, plopped down in a chair, and sobbed.

SIX

Assistance from Victim's Brother Patrick

"Regions Hospital and Adam Brooten, here we come?" Martin asked as he started his unmarked car.

"Correct on both counts. The rush hour traffic won't help. When do you think we'll arrive?"

"The backup on the Lafayette Bridge will slow us down, but we should be there by 7:45."

"And we'll pass headquarters on the way. Too bad I can't drop off my car."

Martin said happily, "Feels great to be working on a case together again, Pete."

Pete smiled and said, "Couldn't agree more, partner."

En route, Pete and Martin discussed their plan of attack. Per their mother, the three oldest children disliked or even hated their father. They, like her, had a motive. Hence, they would interview all four children at headquarters and record the interviews.

Ordinarily, they'd avoid accusations of coercion by having a parent present during interviews of sixteen- and fourteen-year-olds, even though Minnesota law didn't require it. However, this time, it wouldn't happen, and they'd do their best to keep Julie from conferring with her kids prior to the interviews. Chances were too great that she'd interfere with the reliability of the interviews by coaching them, and she remained a suspect.

"You know," Pete said, "since their mother spoke so highly of her brother-in-law, Pat Brooten, maybe he'd be willing to sit in on those interviews, assuming he can fit them into his schedule."

"Julie Brooten will probably be furious if she isn't allowed to be there," Martin said, "but no doubt she'll be happier with Pat than no one."

Pete retrieved the contact information for Pat Brooten and called his cell, hoping.

Pat answered on the second ring, and Pete introduced himself.

Before he could say anything more, Pat said, "I just talked to Julie. She said I should expect to hear from you."

Pete said they needed to meet with him ASAP, but held off on explaining the reason for the rush. "Where are you?" he asked.

"On my way into downtown St. Paul."

"Can my partner and I meet with you now? The meeting will be brief, but we'll talk again later."

"*Hmm.* Mysterious. How soon can you reach my office?"

Pat was on speaker, so Martin flashed five fingers, and Pete relayed that estimate.

Pat said he'd see them shortly, and Pete verified the address Julie had provided.

After disconnecting, in response to Martin's questioning look, Pete explained, "Due to the kind of help we need from Pat and when we'll need it, I think we're better off speaking with him now, ahead of Adam's interview. I hope Pat will help and be able to rearrange his schedule to make himself available for Emily and Sam's interviews. It's already the eleventh hour, but more likely he can work it now than if we wait until after we speak with Adam."

Martin nodded and headed to downtown St. Paul.

Pat Brooten had an office on the eleventh floor in the Bremer Tower. The plaque outside his office said, "Brooten Management Consultants," so the two investigators were surprised when they opened the door and entered an impressively large office with a single, massive, mahogany desk along the back wall. Two large, leather chairs stood in front of it, and a coffee table and four navy-blue wingback chairs hugged the left side of the office.

Pat stood and approached them as they entered. He was a trim and handsome six feet three, had brown hair, and warm brown eyes. He wore a navy suit that exuded dollar signs, a white shirt, and a striped silk tie. After introducing himself, he steered them over to the wingback chairs.

"Since you've spoken with Julie," Pete began, "are we correct in assuming you've heard about your brother, Fred?"

Pat sighed and nodded.

"We'd like to express our sympathy on your loss," Pete said. "In order to save time," he continued, "why don't you tell us what she's told you?"

"Because I'd prefer it the other way around."

Pete understood the logic and said, "Your brother Fred was found shot to death shortly after 5:30 this morning. Were you and he close?"

"We rarely spoke, but let's back up. Julie told me you suspect her and her kids. That's crazy!"

"If you're referring to our meetings with her and their children," Pete said, we always meet with the family. Who is in a better position to tell us about the victim, their friends and enemies, et cetera?"

Pat came forward and almost out of his chair, saying, "I can guarantee none of them did it!"

"Seriously?" Martin asked. "How can you do that? Were you with all five of them and awake from 4:30 until 6:00 this morning?"

"Of course not, but I know all of them, and I know none of them are capable of shooting Fred."

"That won't suffice," Pete said. "Based on our meeting with Julie, you're close to her kids. Because we are currently unable to rule her out as a suspect, we cannot permit her to be present when we interview Emily and Sam. Any way you can be available? Needless to say, you won't be permitted to say or do anything to steer or influence their answers to our questions. If you can be present without doing that, we'd like to have you sit in. We're not yet able to give you an exact time, but it should happen either later this morning or early this afternoon."

After a long pause, Pat nodded and said, "Yes, I can manage that. Will this happen at headquarters?"

"Yes," Pete said. "In another ninety minutes, we should be able to narrow the time frame. If we notify you twenty minutes before each of the two meetings, will that suffice?"

"I'll make it work."

Pete and Martin thanked him and resumed their trip to Regions Hospital.

SEVEN
Victim's Son Adam, APE One

To maximize the chances of success in meeting with Adam Brooten this morning, Pete waited until Martin pulled into the Regions parking lot to call his cell. Since Adam might not dare use his cell during work hours, his backup plan was to get ahold of the head of the sanitation engineers and reach Adam through that person.

The fact that cellphones have caller ID was again a concern. Wondering why a twenty-one-year-old who was on the clock would answer a blocked call, Pete almost dropped his phone when a friendly, deep voice said, "Hello," sounding more like a question than a greeting.

Having Adam answer left Pete wondering if his mother called, shared the news about his dad, and told him to expect a call from the police. There were worse things she could have done, but not many when it came to his and Martin's efforts.

"Adam Brooten?" Pete asked.

"Yes. Who are you?"

Pete explained that he and his partner were investigators with the St. Paul Police Department, and they wanted to meet with him.

"Why?"

"We need your help with an investigation."

"About?"

"I'll explain when we meet."

"Can it wait until after I get off work at 3:00?"

"Sorry, no. Is there someone we should speak with to get permission?"

"Why can't it wait a few hours?"

"It's urgent. Time sensitive. Give me your supervisor's phone number, and I'll arrange it."

"Won't I get docked for the time?"

"If you give me that number, Adam, I think I can keep that from happening. Where can we find you?"

It would have saved time if Adam got his jacket and met them at the Jackson Street entrance, but asking him to do that might cause Adam to bolt. So Pete went the long way around and arranged to meet in front of the cafeteria in five minutes.

Adam asked how he would recognize them.

"Look for two guys in suits and overcoats. That will at least narrow the field."

"I'm six foot three. That will narrow the field too," Adam said.

It didn't sound like Adam had spoken with his mom this morning. That made Pete smile.

The two investigators reached the cafeteria with a minute to spare. While Martin watched for a tall man dressed in the blue work pants and shirts worn by maintenance staff, Pete called Adam's supervisor. He got voicemail and left a message explaining who he was and that Adam would be busy for the next while, assisting with an investigation. He added that he hoped Adam wouldn't be docked for the time, since he was doing a public service.

He'd just completed the call when he heard the soft ring of the elevator. When the doors opened, Pete saw a man about his height but shaped more like a bear exiting it. He had sandy-colored hair, wide shoulders, and huge hands and feet.

He has his dad's hazel eyes, Pete thought. He and Martin had reached the ME crew and the body just before Don closed the victim's empty eyes that stared into nothingness ... or perhaps into Fred's version of eternity.

Pete stepped forward, extended a hand, and asked, "Adam?"

"Yes, sir. Commander Culnane?"

Pete nodded, introduced Martin, and said, "We need your help, Adam. I left a message with your supervisor, and we want you to come to headquarters. No, you're not under arrest," he added, seeing Adam's reaction.

"Can't we meet here?"

"We're in the middle of an investigation, so it's important we have a record of the meeting. That's why we need to do this at headquarters."

Frowning and raising an eyebrow, Adam said, "Are you saying I did something?"

"No," Pete said and added, "Let's get your jacket, stocking cap, and gloves. It's still mighty cold out there."

The two investigators went along while Adam retrieved his outerwear, again guarding against an unobserved exit, then walked with him to the unmarked car.

When they reached HQ, Martin gave Adam a tour, while Pete set up the audio and video recording equipment for Interview Room 1, and bought a Coke and some snacks for Adam. Finally, the three men settled in the room. With the audio and video recording, Pete recited the date and time. He paused, folded his hands, and said, "I'm sorry to have to tell you this, Adam. Your father was attacked this morning and died."

Despite all they'd heard that morning, Pete and Martin were taken aback when a smile flashed across Adam's face, displacing the look of fascination he'd worn since arriving at HQ. But it lasted only a second, before being replaced with a look of contempt as he said, "So you brought me here because you think I killed him?"

Pete stopped Adam before he could say another word and Mirandized him, taking time to insure he understood his rights, including the right to have an attorney present. Then he said, "You were saying, Adam?"

"I was telling you that if you think I killed the old man, you're crazy! I'm not sorry he's gone, but if I was going to kill him, I'd have done it three years ago, before I left home. It sounds cold and disrespectful, but I'm glad. Mom doesn't have to be afraid of him anymore, and I don't have to spend so much time worrying about her."

"Meaning?" Pete asked.

With a voice seething with hatred and words peppered with expletives, Adam said, "I know he hit her more than once in the final months before she kicked him out. It may have started long before I became aware of it. Maybe she was good at hiding the bruises. Or maybe he was careful and only hit her in places that were hidden by her clothes. He was never brave or maybe stupid enough to do it when I was home. At fifteen, I was already six feet tall and a two-hundred-pound weightlifter and wrestler.

"I moved out three years ago, but couldn't have done that had Mom not already thrown him out. Before I moved, I found the best locksmith in the Twin Cities and had him change all the locks and install a security system. The inability to do that would also have forced me to keep living at home. I had a long talk with Mom and begged her not to let him in the house no matter what. I made her promise she wouldn't."

He added, "Then, just in case, I bought her a gun. I told her she had to hide it and promise she would never tell Paul she had it or where she hid it. You see, I was afraid if Paul saw the SOB hit Mom, he'd shoot him if he got his hands on a gun, and then Paul's life would be over. Paul isn't as big as the old man and me, but he hates the bastard just as much as me—or more."

"Is your mother familiar with guns and how to shoot them?" Martin asked.

Adam tilted his head and said, "I doubt it, but I figured the creep would bolt if she pulled one on him."

"What kind of gun did you buy?" Martin asked.

"I have no idea. I know nothing about guns, except they kill people. I bought the first one I could. I wasn't in any position to be choosy. Didn't know if or when I'd have a second chance."

"Caliber?" Martin asked.

"Got me." Adam shrugged. "What difference would it make anyway? A gun is a gun."

"Where did you get it?" Pete asked.

Adam stared at his hands a minute, then said, "I don't remember."

"You know, and we know, that isn't true," Pete said.

Adam closed his eyes, bit his lower lip, then said, "I found it in a park."

"Oh, which park?" Pete asked.

After a long pause, Adam said, "In the Boundary Waters."

"No kidding? When were you there?" Pete asked.

"Just before I gave it to Mom."

"How long were you up there?" Pete asked.

"Almost a week."

"Which entry point did you use?" Pete asked.

"I don't remember. I'm not good with names."

"Where did you stay?" Pete asked.

"At a campground."

"Which one?" Pete asked.

After staring at the wall above Pete's head for several seconds, Adam said, "I can't remember that name either."

"But you stayed at a campground?" Pete asked.

"Sure did."

"I'll bet you remember the names of the lakes you saw, don't you?" Pete asked.

"There were so many."

"I know. Just give me the name of one."

Adam stared at his hands, perhaps hoping for a revelation, then said, "Lake Vermilion."

"Okay, Adam, so far without exception all your answers are wrong. There are no campgrounds, only campsites, and Lake Vermillion is about ninety miles north of Duluth, not in the BWCA. Knock off all the BS and tell us where you got it," Pete said.

"Okay, fine." Adam sighed and ran his hand through his hair. "I needed a gun and was too young to buy one. So I spent a lot of time hanging around outside bars in downtown, telling everyone I was sure couldn't be a police officer that I was looking to buy a gun. After almost a week, I finally found a guy who said he'd give me a good deal on one with a fully loaded 15-round magazine for $350 cash. All I had to do was meet him the next night, a Sunday, at 10:30 at the corner of Albemarle and Nebraska."

Looking up he went on, "I had no idea it would cost that much, but it had already taken a week, and for all I knew it was a good price. So I got there like fifteen minutes early, not taking a chance on missing him. When it was about 10:35 and he hadn't shown, I began thinking he'd been screwing with me. Just when I was about to give up and leave, he showed."

"What was his name?" Pete asked, confident Adam wouldn't have been told.

Adam crossed his arms over his chest and said, "Got me. He never said. I guess he wasn't that stupid, huh?"

"What he look like?" Martin asked.

"It was a cold March night, and he wore a ski mask. He was fairly short. Came only up to my chin and it was hard to tell, because of his down jacket, but it looked like he was pretty roly-poly. That corner wasn't well lit, and I can't describe him any better than that."

"What bar did you meet him in front of?" Martin asked.

"Bob's."

"Before giving the gun to your mom, did you take it to a firing range or out in the country somewhere to test fire it?" Martin asked.

Adam turned red and said, "I should have, shouldn't I. Never thought of it."

"Have you ever fired a gun, Adam?" Martin asked.

Adam shook his head and said, "None of my buddies are into guns."

"How do you get around these days?" Pete asked.

"I bought an old beater."

"Make and model?" Pete asked.

"A Honda Accord. A buddy gave me a good deal on it."

"What color?" Pete asked.

"Black, or maybe I should say black and orange. There's a fair amount of rust on it." Adam smiled, relaxing a bit, now that they were discussing something less threatening.

"Year?" Pete asked.

"2009. Why? Interested?"

"Perhaps in a year or two when my son gets his license." Pete smiled.

"By then, I hope to be in the market for an upgrade." Adam grinned. "Be sure to keep my name and phone number someplace handy and call me. I'll give you a good deal."

Pete nodded and asked, "Have you ever been to your father's condo?"

"He lived in a condo? Last I knew, he lived in a four-bedroom home that was a real dump. I've been waiting for it to burn to the ground—a total loss. That always seemed like something he'd do. Figured he knew all the ins and outs, since he's in the insurance business."

"How do you get to work?" Martin asked.

"Drive. For that reason, I'm glad I start so early. When I arrive, there are still parking spots available on Jackson, north of University."

"What route do you take?" Martin asked.

"Because I arrive before 7:00, I'm ahead of most of the rush-hour traffic. So I take Highway 36 west to I-35E and stay on it all the way to University. I'm also ahead of rush-hour traffic when I leave work. Can't even imagine spending an hour or more commuting each day. I'd either move or find a different job." Adam shook his head and asked, "Where did they get the bastard?"

"If you mean your father, we aren't yet permitted to share the details," Pete said. "Any idea who might have wanted to hurt him?"

"Aside from my family and me? Just so you know, I know none of us killed him."

"How do you know that?"

"Because if we were going to do it, we'd have done it a long time ago, like when he was still living with us."

"How about non-family enemies?" Pete asked.

"Got me. Can't even remember the last time I saw him."

"Who were his friends?" Pete asked.

Adam answered with a hands up shrug and said, "I don't know any of them. When he and Mom were still married, none of them ever came in our house or did anything with our family. Whenever he went out with them and one of them drove, the driver pulled into the driveway and laid on the horn until Dad walked out the door. Either they didn't want anything to do with us, or he didn't want us to have anything to do with them. Or maybe he was embarrassed by or ashamed of us and the house, huh?"

"Are you aware we can arrest you for the illegal purchase of a firearm, Adam?" Pete asked.

"No, but what was I supposed to do? Mom needed the protection."

"If you cooperate in our efforts to find the seller, we'll let it go at that," Martin said.

"I'm happy to help, but I don't know how I can, other than showing you where I met him in downtown and the corner where he sold it to me. I never spoke with him on the phone, and I didn't see his face. I might be able to narrow the field when it comes to his height and shape, if he wears a down jacket and hasn't gained or lost a lot of weight."

Forensics would be contacting Julie, seizing the gun, and checking to see if it was the murder weapon, but Pete saw no sense in sharing that with Adam at this time. He was amazed Julie lied about having any firearms and wondered about her reason for doing so. Did that point the finger at her? At Paul? If so, why was she so forthcoming about the animosity between her and her children and Fred?

Pete stood and said, "That's all for now, Adam. "I'm sorry you didn't have a better relationship with your dad. It was his loss."

"Ditto," Martin said.

"What's your preference? Back to Regions?" Pete asked.

"Yeah. I can walk if you prefer. It's only a few blocks."

"No," Pete said. "Sit tight for a few minutes, and we'll give you a ride."

Martin joined him in his office and asked, "Search warrant?"

Pete nodded and said, "Since she lied about having a gun, we'll have Forensics search her house for it and any other firearms."

It was decision time when it came to how they dealt with Julie. She could be arrested for possessing an illegal firearm, but would they accomplish more by going easy on her, thereby hopefully gaining her cooperation? And no doubt jailing her would affect their ability to get answers from her children. For that reason, other than seizing the gun, they'd do nothing for now.

"Do you want to take Adam back to Regions or take care of the search warrant?" Pete asked."

"I'll give Adam a ride. It won't take long. Then I'll contact Paul's high school and get the School Resource Officer (SRO) to pull him out of class, so we can pick him up and interview him next."

EIGHT
Son Paul, APE Two

Thanks to Adam's disclosure, the search warrant was a slam dunk, requiring little time and even less effort. By the time Martin went to and from Regions and made arrangements with the SRO to pull Paul Brooten surreptitiously out of class, Pete had it and Forensics was preparing to send a team to Julie Brooten's home. After meeting with Adam, Pete and Martin both wondered if their meeting with Paul would be as revealing.

Per the arrangements he'd made with the SRO, Martin waited at the curb in the unmarked car, and Pete followed the directions to the SRO's office and the second Brooten child.

Paul was six feet tall and thin. His dark-brown hair hung down over his forehead, and his hazel eyes peered through black-framed eyeglasses. He wore jeans, a sweatshirt, and Adidas, and shifted nervously from one foot to the other while the SRO introduced him to Pete.

After thanking the SRO for his help, Pete turned to Paul and explained that he and his partner needed Paul's help with an investigation. "For that reason," he said, "we'll go to headquarters, where we'll have a better place to talk."

Paul looked at Pete through the corner of his eye and said, "What's wrong with right here?"

"We discussed that possibility and decided against it," Pete said.

Paul shook his head, grabbed his jacket off the chair he'd been sitting in, and accompanied Pete wordlessly to the unmarked car. He sat hunched in the back seat all the way to HQ.

He'd never met a teenage boy who didn't have a hollow leg. So, hoping to earn some brownie points and get Paul to relax, Pete took a roundabout path to Interview Room 1, passing the snack machines. Then he stopped, said he wanted some peanuts, and asked if he could get Paul anything.

"I could use a Coke," Paul said.

"And?" Pete asked.

"Chips too?"

"You can get anything you want, until I run out of cash."

Paul looked at him as if he was Santa Claus and selected peanut M&Ms.

"That's it?"

So Paul also got Cheetos and a granola bar. Then looking at Pete, he grinned and said, "I hope I won't need to be here any longer than it takes to eat all this."

"If so, we can take a break and return for seconds." Pete smiled.

Martin was waiting for them at the same interview room where they met with Adam, and he motioned Paul over to the chair facing the door.

Paul walked around the table, arranged his haul on the table in front of him, and sat down. He opened the Coke, took a drink, opened the Cheetos, and only then looked up at Martin and Pete.

Repeating what he'd said to Adam, Pete told Paul his father was attacked this morning and died.

Paul rolled his eyes and said, "Good joke. What am I really doing here?"

"We need your help in determining what happened to him," Martin said.

Paul looked stunned and said, "Wait! He's really dead?"

Martin nodded and said, "Yes, I'm sorry."

"No need to feel bad about it." After a long pause, he added, "So how can I help?"

"When did you last see your dad?" Martin asked.

Paul looked pensive. After a long pause he said, "It has to be more than a year. I got a really dumb birthday card from him last June, but didn't see him. It has to be at least a year and maybe two."

"So you weren't close?" Pete asked.

"That's actually laughable. I've hated him for as long as I can remember. I was only twelve, but I can't even tell you how happy I was when Mom threw him out. I think it was the best thing she could do for all of us."

"Why did you hate him, Paul?" Pete asked.

"He treated Mom and us kids like garbage. He thought we were there to serve him, and nothing we did was ever good enough. He thought he knew it all, and that the rest of us were idiots if we disagreed. He berated all of us and drove my friends away."

"Was he ever physically abusive?" Pete asked.

"He pushed me around, but I don't think that counts. If he was physically abusive to the rest of the family, I never knew about it."

"What time did you get up this morning?"

"At the usual time, 6:45. Do you think I killed him?"

Pete held up both hands, palms out, and said, "Hang on a minute." He hated to stop him now, because Paul might then clam up, but he couldn't risk having him blurt out a confession before he'd been Mirandized, unlikely as it seemed. So he jumped in before Paul could say anything else and asked if he had heard of the Miranda warning.

Paul nodded and said, "So you do think I did it, don't you."

"No," Pete said, "but we're obligated to inform you of your rights before you say anything else. It protects you and us."

Paul rolled his eyes, then listened while Pete read the Miranda warning, explained it, and asked if he wanted an attorney.

Paul shook his head and said, "No, I want to finish here and get back to school before I miss any more classes." Then he signed the statement, popped a couple of M&Ms in his mouth and asked, "Where were we, before you got so paranoid?"

Pete hid a smile and said, "You were asking if we thought you killed your father."

"Oh yeah," Paul nodded. "Before the timeout, I was about to say that there were a lot of times when I avoided him, was angry and embarrassed that he was such a jerk, wanted him out of the house and out of my life. But kill him? No."

"Who might have wanted to kill him?" Pete asked.

Paul counted them off on his fingers as he said, "Adam, maybe, but I know he didn't. Mom, but she wouldn't have the wherewithal. Emily couldn't pull it off either. And it would never occur to Sam. He still likes the jerk. Don't ask me why. It makes no sense. Maybe it's a baby of the family syndrome."

"How about people outside your immediate family?" Pete asked.

"He worked with a lot of people, but when he lived with us, I don't think any of them came over, and I don't think he did anything with them after work. My friends all do things with their dads and their dads' friends. Not me. I never went anywhere with him or saw him with other people. If he had friends or enemies, I never met them. You should ask Mom."

Both investigators watched his facial expressions. If Paul felt grief or any sense of loss, he did a great job of hiding it.

Then Martin slipped away to arrange a few other things, and Pete continued the questioning. "Have you ever tested your aim, like at a firing range, say with friends?"

"No, none of my friends do that stuff."

"But you've probably held a gun, say one that belonged to a friend's dad."

"Is that how he was killed? Someone shot him?"

"Just answer my question, Paul."

"No, never held one or even wanted to."

"Was your mom afraid of your dad?"

"I think she dreaded hearing from him, but I don't think she was afraid of him."

"Did she do anything to protect herself, just in case?" Pete asked.

Paul stared into space for several seconds, then said, "Adam had the locks changed and a security system installed after she threw him out. I don't know of anything else ... and she didn't really do those things."

Pete thanked Paul for his cooperation and asked if he still wanted to go back to school. "A meeting like this can take the starch out of a guy," he added.

Paul laughed and said, "That's a good one. I'll have to remember it. I have a test in a few hours and don't want to have to take it later."

Pete gave him a business card, in case he thought of anything else.

Paul nodded, then said, "I probably shouldn't tell you this, but I kind of hope you don't catch the person. They did me and my family a favor. But I won't do anything to impede your investigation. I know solving cases is important to people like you."

"Hang tight," Pete said. "I'll be back in a few minutes, and we'll take you back to school. Meanwhile, need anything from the vending machines?"

Paul put a hand on his stomach and said, "Thanks, but I think I'm about to suffer from a sugar overload."

While Pete was finishing up with Paul, Martin was in Pete's office, on the phone with the same SRO at the high school. He was working on a plan to pick up Emily, until he learned she had a test in a few minutes. So he told the SRO he'd be back in touch in about an hour. Then he called the SRO at Sam's middle school and arranged to pick Sam up in about thirty minutes. Finally, he called Pat Brooten and asked him to meet them at HQ in a half hour.

Pete walked in as Martin disconnected from that last call, and Martin told him about the arrangements. Then they returned to Interview Room 1, got Paul, and drove a more-talkative passenger back to the high school.

Paul thanked them for the ride, but said nothing about the interview, and hurried to the entrance.

Thankfully, the middle school wasn't far away.

NINE
Victim's Son Sam, APE Four

Pete and Martin repeated the process they'd followed when picking up Paul, and Pete found Sam Brooten in the SRO's office. He looked happy to be anywhere but in class, and he jumped up and smiled when Pete introduced himself.

Sam was a skinny five foot three with untamed, thick brown hair and big blue eyes. He wore blue jeans, a gray hooded parka, unzipped to reveal a yellow T-shirt emblazed with a Billie Eilish logo, and Nikes.

He was nothing like Paul. He talked about school, baseball, and band all the way to the unmarked car. Once inside, he switched to a running narrative about cars and trucks, and what he was going to buy as soon as he turned sixteen.

Pat hadn't arrived at HQ yet, so Martin waited for him inside the main entrance. He wanted to provide a brief orientation, including the likelihood they'd Mirandize Sam and why, before they hooked up with Pete and Sam.

Once again, Pete took a detour past the vending machines on the way to Interview Room 1. Stopping in

front of the machines he said, "Hungry, Sam?" He'd yet
to meet a fourteen-year-old who wasn't a bottomless pit.

"Yes, sir, but I don't have any money. Already spent
my allowance."

Reaching into his pocket, Pete pulled out a handful
of coins. "Hold out your hands," he said, then
transferred the coins to Sam.

"You guys are really nice," Sam said, sounding
amazed. He bought a full-strength Coke and studied the
machines before selecting a bag of Fritos.

"Are you sure that'll suffice?" Pete asked and added,
"This could take awhile."

"You won't mind?" Sam asked, eyebrows raised.

"Heck no. Help yourself."

This time the selection took no time. Sam chose
Oreos. Then he held out the hand still loaded with coins
to Pete.

"Keep it, Sam. You never know when hunger will
strike."

When they reached the interview room, Martin and
Pat Brooten were already there. Sam saw his uncle, ran
over to him, and gave him a hug. "I didn't know you
were coming," he said. "This is as good as Christmas!"

Pat sat next to Sam, and Pete and Martin sat across
the table from them.

After announcing the date and time, and while Sam
was opening the Coke and digging into the Fritos, Pete
began by saying, "Looks like you're a Nike fan, Sam. Are
you? Or is it a coincidence you're wearing their shoes?"

Sam paused the migration of the Coke to his mouth
and said, "I love them, but rarely get them. Mom says
they are usually too exorbitant. I tried telling her it's
worth it when they make me run faster, jump higher, and
stop quicker." Sam smiled.

A victim of the advertising age, Pete thought.

"We'd better get down to business," Pete said. "I'm sorry to have to tell you this, Sam. Your dad died this morning."

Sam gasped in pain and shock, slumped and his head dropped. "He had a heart attack?" he asked. "Mom said he'd have one if he didn't lose at least fifty pounds."

"No." Pete said. "Someone attacked him."

Eyes wide, Sam looked up. "Where? When? Who would do that?"

"It happened early this morning," Pete said. "We're doing our best to determine who did it and why, and we hope you'll be able to help."

"Do you have any idea who might want to hurt him, Sam?" Martin asked.

Lips trembling, eyes closed, Sam shook his head. "We were going to go see the Twins play this spring," he said as tears flowed down his cheeks.

Martin pushed a box of tissues toward him.

Pat moved his chair in close and put an arm around Sam's shoulders.

"If he had enemies, you didn't know about them?" Martin asked.

Staring at the table, Sam again shook his head.

"He never mentioned having problems with neighbors or the people he worked with, anyone like that?" Martin asked.

After a long pause, Sam said, "He often complained about the idiots and the jerks he had to work with, but I don't think he ever mentioned their names. And I remember he got mad when a neighbor said our grass was too long. You *have to* find the person who killed him! And life in prison will be too good for them. They should be electrocuted, given a lethal injection, or whatever we do in Minnesota. Please, you have to find out who did it and catch them. He was my dad, and I'll never ever again be with him. It isn't fair!"

Sam put his head onto his arms on the table and his back shook with sobs.

Pat put a hand on Sam's back and patted it.

Pete waited until Sam stopped shaking, then asked, "When did you last see your dad, Sam?"

"Martin Luther King's birthday. We didn't have school, but Mom had to work. He called the house and Emily answered. He must have changed his voice, 'cause she didn't know it was him. He asked for me, and we decided to meet a couple of blocks from home. He said he couldn't pick me up at home, because Mom wanted to hurt him. I don't know why she hates him, but I know she does. I wish Dad never moved out. It made seeing him so much harder. I almost never see him, and now ..." *Sob*.

"How did your brothers and your sister feel about him?" Martin asked.

"Adam and Emily seem to hate him. Paul pretends he doesn't exist. They didn't understand him the way I do ... But they wouldn't hurt him. They wouldn't do that to me, 'cause they know I love him."

"When your mom and dad got divorced, did you have a choice which one you'd live with?" Pete asked.

Eyes closed, Sam nodded like a bobblehead doll.

"And you chose your mom?" Pete asked.

"Yeah. That was a mistake, huh? I was only eight, I didn't want to be alone while getting ready for school after Dad went to work, and I didn't want to be alone until he got home at night. I was in a school with all my friends, and I didn't want to go to a new school and try to make all new friends. I might almost never see Adam,

Paul, and Emily, and I was afraid Mom wouldn't love me anymore if I chose Dad." Sam wailed.

"You were an incredible eight year old to think of all those things and make such a good choice, Sam. I'm impressed," Pete said.

"Me too, Sam," Martin said. You're amazing."

"But it was the wrong choice. While we talked on the phone often, I hardly ever saw him, and now I never will again." Sam buried his head in his arms and cried silently.

Pat pulled Sam's chair back from the table, lifted his shoulders up off it, and held him in his arms until Sam's back stopped shaking.

Pete regretted being unable to have Sam's mom there with them, but still believed it was the right decision. *Thank goodness his uncle, Pat, is here*, he thought. Feeling powerless, he asked Sam if there was anything he could do to help.

Head buried in Pat's shoulder, Sam shook it almost imperceptibly.

He seems lost, Pete thought. Driven to help in some way, he broke the silence, attacking Sam's loss in a way he'd hoped Pat would.

Starting slow, giving Pat time to take over, he said something he'd hoped Pat would say, "Do you believe in heaven, Sam?"

Sam nodded slowly.

After glancing at Pat and seeing only a look of surprise, he continued. "Me too, and that helps me a lot when someone I love dies, because it means I will see them again. You know, your dad is probably looking down on you from heaven right now. I'll bet it's breaking his heart to see you so sad. I'll bet he wants nothing more than to help you feel better. I know I'd feel that way if I was him.

"I have a brand new son. One day I'd like to take him to Target Field to see the Twins play," Pete said and looked at Pat.

Pat hugged Sam a little tighter and said, "Would you go to Target Field with me this spring, Sam?"

Resurrecting himself from Pat's shoulder, Sam said, "You'd do that?"

"I'd love to do that. We can sit there and drink pop, eat hot dogs and peanuts, and scream our lungs out. What do you say?"

Looking astonished, Sam nodded.

While Martin called forensics, Pete, Pat, and Sam talked about their favorite Twins players, the best games ever, who was going to win the 2019 World Series, and everything baseball.

Meanwhile, Martin learned that Forensics was wrapping up their search of Julie Brooten's home. They found a 9 mm Smith and Wesson M&P Shield Plus with a fully loaded ten-round magazine, seized it, and found no other firearms. It would be a few hours before they knew if it was the weapon used to murder Fred. And Martin needn't worry if he wanted to send the youngest child home. They'd be gone before he arrived.

Martin was worried about Julie's emotional state, after Forensics arrived without warning and searched her home. So he called her next, wondering if she was in any emotional state to deal with a distraught son. They still didn't know whether she'd murdered or participated in the murder of her ex, but he was certain she'd never hurt one of her kids.

Julie exploded when he told her they had spoken with Sam and told him about his dad. But she calmed down when she learned why he'd called, said she'd already called in sick, and asked him to please bring Sam home.

Relieved, Martin arranged to have Pat take Sam home and return immediately to be there for their meeting with Emily.

Lastly, he reconnected with the SRO at the high school and arranged to pick up Emily in about twenty minutes.

TEN
Daughter Emily, APE Three

Sticking with the system that worked well twice, Martin stayed in the car while Pete went into the school for Emily Brooten.

When he reached the SRO's office, Pete discovered either Emily Brooten hadn't inherited her parents' genes for well-above-average height or her growth spurt had yet to kick in. She was only five feet four. Emily was slim and athletic-looking like her mom, with shoulder-length, wavy brown hair, bright blue eyes, a small nose, and full lips. She wore what appeared to be the uniform for girls her age, consisting of leggings, a puffer jacket, an oversized hoodie, and Converse tennis shoes. Arms crossed, she stood just inside the SRO's office, working on her bored teenager look.

Pete walked over to her, showed her his ID, then extended a hand.

"What's the deal? This has to be the craziest day ever. Why am I here and not in class?"

"My partner and I need your help with an investigation. He's waiting in the car. We'll go to my office and bring you back as fast as we can."

Under protest, they joined Martin in the unmarked car, and Pete introduced Emily.

Prior to picking her up, Pete opened a roll of quarters and deposited them in a trouser pocket. Again he attempted to use the vending machines as an ice breaker. It seemed he'd get less mileage out of it this time. All Emily wanted was a bottle of water.

Martin and Pat weren't there yet when they reached Interview Room 1, so Pete showed Emily where to sit and left to check on them. He barely exited the room when he saw them coming around the corner.

Like Sam, Emily was pleased to see her uncle, but less vocal about it.

Once everyone was seated, Pete went through the preliminaries, including explaining they would record the meeting. He explained that this was standard procedure, and they could take a break whenever Emily or Pat wanted. Then he announced the date and time.

This time Martin shared the news about Frederick Brooten.

Emily bit her lip, stared at him, and said, "Are you saying someone killed my dad? Are you sure you have the right guy?"

Martin nodded and said they had positive identification. There was no mistake.

"But why would someone kill him?"

"That's why we pulled you out of school," Pete said. "We hope you can help us determine that. Did your dad have any enemies that you knew of?"

Emily shook her head and said, "I haven't seen him around other people for years. He stopped by the house sometimes when Mom was at work, but it was just us and him."

"Were the two of you on close terms?" Pete asked.

Emily sighed and said, "Actually, no. He thought he had the right to order us kids around, and I no longer need anyone telling me what to think and what to do."

"Did he ever talk about his relationships with other people, such as the people he worked with, his neighbors, anyone like that? Did he ever mention being mad at someone or someone being mad at him?"

"He often talked about the stupidity of the people he worked with. He moved a while back, and he said a lot of his new neighbors didn't have the brains of a walnut. He tended to be pretty impatient with everybody. He never said he was mad at anyone or anyone at him."

"When he came to see you, did he ever take you places?" Martin asked.

Emily shook her head and said, "There was never ever enough time. He'd call first, then stop on his way home from work. Once he left just before you arrived, Uncle Pat." Emily glanced over at him. "That wouldn't have been good, would it," she said, still looking at him. "You knew Mom didn't want him coming over. I know you'd never kill him, but did you hate him, Pat?" Her eyes grew moist.

Pat squeezed her hand and said, "He was my brother. I loved him, Emily, but I didn't like him."

"Your mom is mighty busy, isn't she?" Pete asked.

"Yeah. I wish she didn't have to work so much." Emily frowned.

"Do you think she'd like to get married again some day?" Pete asked, wishing Pat wasn't here for this line of questioning about his sister-in-law and wondering if his presence would affect Emily's answers.

Emily nodded and said, "Definitely."

"She meets a lot of people through work. Does she ever talk about any of them?" Pete asked.

"Yeah, there's this one guy I think she kind of likes. I keep telling her she should start dating."

"And what does she say?" Martin asked.

"She asked where she'd find the time. I told her that Paul, Sam, and I can take care of ourselves, and she can go out after work. She doesn't work *that* late. When she said she had to get up too early in the morning to go out after work, I told her that, when she did, I could get up a little earlier and get Sam out the door to school."

"What did she say to that?" Martin asked.

"I think she's thinking about it. I hope she does." Emily looked pensive, opened her bottle of water, and took a sip.

"Did she tell you his name?" Martin asked, planning on adding it to the list of suspects.

Emily nodded and said, "It's Jamison Revere. I told her he could be related to Paul Revere. Wouldn't that be awesome? If they got married and he adopted me, I would be Emily Revere, and my initials would be ER. Nice, huh? Of course, I haven't told Mom. She's said she hasn't even dated him, and I already have her married. I want her to be happy. I don't think she was happy when she and Dad were married."

"Why is that?" Pete asked.

"He wasn't very nice to her. He yelled at her a lot, and he criticized everything she did. I was glad when they got divorced. Things got better for all of us, once he moved out."

"How did they get better for you, Emily?" Pete asked.

"Well, Dad yelled at me too, and he was always telling me I had to study more and spend less time with my friends. He used to upset Adam and Paul a lot, and he was always yelling at them too. I don't know how to explain it, except to say the atmosphere got calmer, happier, and less stressful after he moved. I wish it hadn't had to be that way." Emily sighed.

Pete and Martin thanked her and gave her their business cards, asking her to call if she thought of anything else. Then Pete asked if she wanted to go home or back to school. "If you want to confer with your mom before deciding," he said, "you can use one of our phones."

She did and after speaking with her mom decided to go home.

Pete and Martin would save some time by getting another investigator to drive her home, but they decided against it. She now seemed comfortable with them, and how would she feel about being subjected to yet another stranger at a time like this? So they arranged to meet with Pat at his office as soon as they got back to St. Paul.

As Martin pulled into her mom's driveway, Emily reiterated her hopes they would find the person who killed her dad.

"The impacts of a failed marriage," Martin said as he and Pete walked back to the unmarked car to head for downtown St. Paul.

ELEVEN
Back to Brother Pat

Pat Brooten had already spent several hours assisting Pete and Martin, and they were appreciative. Now they wanted to ask him many of the questions they'd asked his niece and nephew. And, because he'd known the deceased longer than anyone, they wanted Pat to tell them about his brother. Already convinced that Pat hadn't murdered Fred, they'd speak with him at his office, rather than in an interview room at headquarters.

Once again, Pat directed the two investigators to the wingback chairs, and Pete began, "Please give us your perspective on Fred."

Pat bent forward, rested his elbows on his knees, and said, "For as long as I can remember, I've hoped Fred would get his life on track before it was too late. Unless something dramatic happened in the last few days, my prayers went unanswered."

Shaking his head, he continued, "I'm sorry to say that my brother was an egotistical, controlling narcissist and bully. He seemed to believe someone died and made him God. Frankly, I'm surprised he made it this far.

"He did his best to ignore his child support responsibilities, and it's always been hard on Pam and their kids. He ignored their needs and recently blew an atrocious sum on a new truck. I have no idea how he pulled it off. Saving was foreign to him, so he must have put down the minimum. Maybe he needed to replace his old truck, but buying something that expensive was crazy. He must have wanted a new toy. I only know about that truck, because he passed me on the road a few days ago. Through some friends, I checked on him and found out he recently got a raise. I called Julie right away and suggested she get an increase in child support. I figured if he could buy a truck like that, the least he could do was make her life a bit easier.

"I tried, repeatedly, to get through to Fred. He didn't care what he was doing to his family financially or emotionally. In fact, I think he enjoyed seeing how much he could get away with. I once said to him 'when all is said and done, that won't be the score that counts.' He insisted that I wasn't qualified to have an opinion, since I was single and child-free. I said this was about being a decent and honorable human being. He thought that was hilarious."

Pat sighed, shook his head and said, "I regret not knowing about his plans to marry Julie in time to convince her it would be a mistake. They married the day I graduated from Harvard, and I didn't find out about it until I returned to Minnesota. I still can't imagine how he put on a good-enough show to convince her to marry him. It still breaks my heart."

"How could you not know about the wedding?" Martin asked. "Surely your dad or your brother would have told you."

"Fred and I hadn't communicated since I'd left to pursue my MBA. We had nothing in common. I thought he was a total loser. Dad and I spoke only when I called him. I got Dad, Steve, and his wife Barb tickets for my graduation. Dad said he'd be there if it worked out. It didn't, of course. Dad was at Fred's wedding, but Steve and Barb showed up to see me graduate. I found out later that Steve, like me, was unaware of Fred's wedding plans."

Pete said, "Julie told us that Steve died in a car accident. But we may want to contact Barb. Do you have her phone number?"

"No," Pat frowned. "Barb was diagnosed with cancer a year or so before Steve's fatal accident, and she died a little more than a year after he did. They were deeply in love, and I've always wondered if she lost her will to live ... stopped fighting the cancer."

"Any idea who might have had a reason to kill Fred?" Martin asked. "Anyone he'd irritated or infuriated enough? Anyone who hated him?"

"Frankly, off the top, because of the way he operated, a majority of the people who dealt with him were likely motivated. But it takes more than a motive, doesn't it? I'll need some time to think about it. The thing is, I've had nothing to do with him since he and Julie divorced. For that reason, I have no idea who he's irritated in the last five or six years."

"Who were his friends?" Pete asked.

"I can't give you a single name. As far as I know, he had no lasting friendships. Most of us have at least a friend or two with whom we've been friends for a decade or more. But Fred went through friends faster than I go through a pair of hiking boots. He hung around with guys similar to him, guys who might help him achieve whatever he was after at the time. I don't think Fred ever got to know the people he hung around with, and I don't think he ever had a deep friendship. How sad is that?"

Looking at Martin, he added, "I assume you asked Emily about anyone interested in Julie, thinking someone might have 'eliminated' Fred as a favor to her?" He smiled.

"Well," Pete stood and said, "thank you for helping us when we needed someone to sit in for Julie, and we appreciate the way you handled it."

"I'm glad it worked out, and I hope you find the person," Pat said, walking them to the door.

On their way to the elevator, Martin said, "Next?"

Looking at his watch, Pete said, "It's 12:30. The doctor who discovered Brooten's body said she'd be available from 11:00 until 1:30. I'll call and make sure this is a good time for her. Dr. Ruth Kinney might be able to provide additional information about what she saw when she came across the crime scene this morning."

TWELVE
Dr. Ruth, Good Samaritan

Dr. Ruth Kinney answered, and told Pete she was available and anxious to meet with them. They arranged to meet at the Jackson Street entrance in five minutes.

"I'll head there now, and I'm wearing a white jacket," she said. "Have to maintain the stereotype." She chuckled.

When they reached Regions, Martin parked along the driveway outside the Jackson Street entrance. Pete minimized the chances their unmarked car would be towed by placing the St. Paul PD plaque on the dashboard.

They found Dr. Kinney standing just inside the revolving door and exchanged introductions.

"What a day," she said after they settled in the privacy of her office. "It went from finding a body on my way in this morning to a simple surgery that became more complex than I could ever have anticipated. Thankfully, the patient survived. I assume you want to know how things unfolded as I approached the scene?"

"Please," Pete said.

"I was heading south on Jackson and still about a half block from Maryland when I saw a truck stopped in my lane. There was a car stopped alongside it and pointed in the same direction. I wondered why the second vehicle stopped in the middle of the oncoming lane, and considered whether there was enough room on either shoulder for me to get around them.

"As my headlights illuminated the area, suddenly I saw someone on the driver's side of the second vehicle. They got in that car and sped through the Maryland intersection. The light was red so that, of course, raised my curiosity and my suspicions. That's when I noticed something that looked like it could be a person lying near the sidewalk in front of the Troutbrook Nature Sanctuary parking lot. It had been blocked from view by the car that sped away.

"I jumped out of my car, and ran to check it out. It was a person lying face down, stretched out like he was trying to reach for something.

"I crouched down and asked a couple of times, 'Can you hear me? There was no response. I touched the side of the man's face. It was cold. That meant little, given the air temperature. So I carefully slid a hand down the side of the face to his neck, looking for a pulse in the carotid artery. The neck was warm, and that was a hopeful sign, but I knew it might only be due to the warmth maintained by the down jacket. I tried and tried, but failed to find a pulse. So I called 911."

Doctor Kinney added, "I know the car that took off was an older model, a 2010 or older, and it was black, navy, or other dark color. I realize that's far too general. Wish I could be more specific. The license plate was so dirty, I couldn't read it. The person who took off could have been a man or a woman. Other than from the shoulders up, the person was hidden by the car they drove. All I saw was what looked like a bulky, down jacket, and a hood pulled around their face. What else can I tell you?"

"Do you remember the taillights?" Martin asked. "That might narrow down the possibilities."

"I think they were rectangular, but I don't remember anything distinct about them. Everything happened so fast, and I didn't pay much attention to that."

"Understood. We appreciate the fact you tried to help the victim, called 911, and made yourself available to answer our questions. Your description of the car that took off might be helpful, depending on what the people we question drive. Regardless, every detail is important. Thanks."

The doctor replied, "And thank you for your efforts and your service to St. Paul, detectives. It's nice having people like you looking out for people like me. I hope you solve this one ... and all your cases."

On their way back to the car, Martin commented, "The world could use more people like her."

His cell vibrated as he opened the car door, and he read the text as soon as he got behind the wheel. It was Forensics. They had compared the markings and striations on the casings found at the crime scene to those made by the gun seized at Julie Brooten's home.

THIRTEEN
Victim's Employer, Fundamentals Insurance

Per the text from Forensics, the gun Adam Brooten bought illegally was not the murder weapon.

Martin handed his phone to Pete, who read the message and said, "Too bad it will take a lot more than that to disqualify the family members as suspects."

"Both neighbors and Brooten's employer and coworkers seem like the logical next steps," he added. "Do you have a preference, Martin?"

Checking the time, Martin said, "It's almost 1:00. Since we aren't far from where he worked, let's start there. It's impossible to know their schedules, but at least some of his fellow employees should be around. Most of his neighbors are probably at work."

Fundamentals Insurance had offices in the Wells Fargo Building in downtown St. Paul.

Martin found all kinds of parking spaces on Seventh Street, between Cedar and Minnesota Streets. He knew all the meters maxed out at fifteen minutes. So he smiled, knowing the St. Paul PD wouldn't ticket his unmarked car.

The temperature had risen to a balmy 34° F, so they left their stocking caps and gloves in the car, and didn't button their overcoats before walking from the car to the entrance.

The directory indicated Fundamentals Insurance on the sixth floor, so they took an elevator up and followed the signs to the insurance company's offices. A receptionist sat inside a glass-fronted cubicle, ready to welcome visitors and control their access to the offices. He greeted Pete and Martin and asked how he could help.

"I understand Frederick Brooten works here," Pete said.

"Yes, sir, but he's not available right now."

Pete and Martin displayed their IDs, and Pete said, "We'd like to speak to his supervisor."

"Hang on, I'll call him," he said and hurriedly punched some numbers on his phone. When the person answered, he said, "There are a couple of police officers out here, asking about Mr. Brooten."

He hung up, smiled, and said, "It will be just a minute."

A plump man in his sixties, of average height if he stood on his tiptoes, walked through the door separating the two investigators from the Fundamentals Insurance employees. He wore khakis, and his dress shirt was open at the collar. He introduced himself as Joe Hardwick and said he was Fred Brooten's supervisor.

When Martin said they had questions about Fred Brooten and his job, Hardwick said it would be better if they spoke with Frederick.

"We'd like to speak with you *about* him," Martin clarified in a tone that left no room for discussion.

"In that case, let's go to my office."

He led the two investigators through the security door and through a sizable room loaded with row upon row of cubicles. Along the far wall were eight offices adorned with name plaques. One said, "Frederick Brooten." Another displayed Hardwick's name. The offices were separated by large rooms labeled Meeting Room One through Seven.

As they walked, Joe explained, "We occupy three floors. Our officers are one floor up, and accounting is down one floor. In broad terms, each floor indicates the office hierarchy."

Once they were seated in his office, Hardwick said, "Frederick is a senior claims adjuster."

"And?" Martin asked.

"In addition to his normal duties, he has been training and breaking in some new claims adjusters. I'm afraid he didn't come in or call this morning. That isn't like him. We're concerned, because he had several appointments."

"I'm sorry to say, Fred was attacked and died early this morning," Martin said.

Hardwick's jaw dropped. After several seconds, he recovered enough to ask, "Attacked? What happened?"

"For now, we're unable to tell you any more than that," Martin said. Then he asked, "What time did he usually arrive?"

"Fred was always the first one in. That's probably why he was so good. All of our employees have IDs that get them in and log their comings and goings. With rare exceptions, Fred was here by 5:30. He said he accomplished more in the ninety minutes before anyone else arrived than he did the rest of the morning."

Still looking shaken, Hardwick added, "He's really going to be missed."

"You probably knew Fred better than anyone here," Pete said. "Tell us about him."

"He was the model of expertise and efficiency. That's why we decided to have him train new adjusters. It wasn't the norm, but we'd hoped some of his work habits, expertise, and techniques would rub off on them."

Pete asked, "Who were his enemies, had problems with him, was angry with him, et cetera?"

"You mean, , who might have killed him?"

"Not necessarily to that level," Pete replied.

Joe closed his eyes, rubbed his chin and said, "Fred was so intense and driven that he sometimes irritated a few people. But I don't think he had any enemies, and I can't imagine who'd want to hurt him."

Martin commented, "I'd be surprised if a claims adjuster didn't sometimes irritate the people whose claims he settled."

"That goes without saying, but I'm confident that would never lead to murder. Or do you think the person might not have meant to kill him?"

"As I said, we're unable to discuss the details at this time," answered Martin.

Hardwick sighed and said, "All I can tell you is, claims adjusters don't get hazardous duty pay. And I've never heard of a dissatisfied claimant killing the adjuster. Lucky thing. We'd have to pay adjusters a lot more."

Martin asked, "Is parking included in the pay package for your employees?"

"No, but we negotiated a discount for them at the World Trade Center ramp."

"Not at the Wells Fargo ramp?" Pete asked.

"No, that's considered a pretty elite place to park."

"Why is that?" Pete asked.

"It's handier, and maybe because, for a fee, you can get your car washed while you work."

"Where do you park?" Martin asked.

Hardwick's face reddened as he said, "At the Wells Fargo ramp."

"What do you drive?" Martin asked, confident it wasn't the older vehicle Dr. Kinney saw racing away from the crime scene.

"A Lexus ES." Hardwick beamed.

"Did Fred act differently the last several days?" Pete asked. "What I mean is, was he more nervous, irritable, anxious, angry, or did he act in any way that was unusual for him?"

"Not that I noticed."

"How much time did you spend with him yesterday?" Pete asked.

"I'd guess thirty-five or forty-five minutes, but it was broken up into a lot of small segments."

"Were you and Fred friends?" Martin asked.

"Of course."

"So you did things together after work," Martin said.

"Well, no. But we were friends."

"Did you ever get together after work?"

Hardwick rearranged some of the papers on his desk and said, "Not that I remember."

Pete said, "We need a list of all the claims, including all the contact information Mr. Brooten and his staff were currently working on, settled, or were involved in the settlement of, for the last three years."

"You're kidding, right?" Hardwick frowned.

"No. The murder of a claims adjuster may be unheard of, but when a guy is liked and respected by everyone, we have to look everywhere possible for an explanation."

"That's going to take some time," Hardwick mumbled.

"In this day of computers?" Pete asked, eyebrows raised. "I'm sure you're exaggerating. Email it to me by the close of business today and carbon copy my partner."

Pete and Martin handed him their business cards and, without giving Hardwick a chance to protest, Pete continued, "We're interested in meeting with the other people who knew him the best."

"Most of his coworkers are out of the office today. But recently he spent much of his time with the three people he was training in, and they're available. Now I'm going to have to figure out what to do with them." Hardwick sighed.

"We'll meet with them, one at a time," Pete said.

Hardwick explained there were several, currently unoccupied meeting rooms they could use and led them into Meeting Room Six. He told them to make themselves comfortable, while he went to get a member of Brooten's staff.

Seeing that windows filled one wall of the room, it occurred to Pete that there were no windows in the room with cubicles. A huge, oak table surrounded by padded leather chairs left room only for a cupboard, holding a coffee maker, cups, cream, and sugar.

The two investigators seated themselves at the head of the table and across the table from the door, insuring that they had the best views of the people they interviewed. While waiting for the arrival of the first, they discussed their game plan in hushed tones.

He may have understood what they were doing, because Joe knocked on the door before entering. Following close on his heels was a gangly man wearing khakis, a turtleneck, and a V-neck sweater. He looked like he was still in his teens.

"This is Carter Jordan," Joe said. "He's the newest member of Fred's staff. I told him and the others about Fred. I hope that's okay."

Both Pete and Martin nodded.

"Carter started late last fall. That was about six weeks after the departure of an original member of Fred's staff. When you're finished with Carter, he'll get one of the other two for you. I'd appreciate speaking with you before you leave. Do you want coffee?"

Pete and Martin thanked him and declined the offer.

Joe nodded and left.

They introduced themselves to Carter, who said, "I can't believe Mr. Brooten is dead. It doesn't seem possible. He was always so full of life, so energetic."

"How did you like working for him?" Martin asked.

"I liked it a lot. I was learning so much, and he never got on my back when I made a mistake. I think that's the only reason I'm still here. He was so patient and understanding. He told me he made at least as many mistakes as I made when he was getting started. He's the one who hired me. I had to meet with three people in his section, and he told me he was the only one of them who picked me. I never do well in interviews, and had spent months trying to land a job. I was getting desperate."

Looking sad, Carter continued, "He took me along on some of his inspections, showed me all the things to watch for, how to know if a claimant was overstating losses, and how important it is to make sure a claimant isn't accidentally overlooking any losses. He showed me a couple of claims where that was the case, and the claimant got a much better settlement, thanks to his diligence. The claimants were, of course, thrilled and so grateful. I told him I was surprised that he didn't figure it was the claimant's responsibility, and he'd save the company money by overlooking the things the claimant missed. He told me I couldn't do that, because it was unethical. I really respected him. Can't believe he's gone. Hope my next supervisor is as good ... and as patient."

Carter had started working for Brooten at the end of November, thought Brooten got along well with all the employees and the claimants, and didn't think he had any enemies.

"Why did a member of his staff leave?" Pete asked.

"I don't know. I asked the other people who work for him, and they'd just shrugged, wouldn't talk about it. I wonder if he found a better job, and Mr. Brooten was angry about that."

Carter hadn't noticed any differences in the way Brooten acted or treated him recently.

They thanked Carter for his assistance and dismissed him.

As he was leaving, Pete said, "By the way, Carter, what kind of car do you drive?"

"A Chevy Impala. Dad and Mom gave it to me as a graduation gift."

"Nice," Pete said. "What color?"

"Chevrolet calls it iridescent pearl tricoat." Carter grinned.

Their next interviewee was Kurt Worthington, who was quick to point out it was Kurt with a "K," not a "C." On the tall side of average and of average build with auburn hair and intense green eyes, he wore a suit and tie. He exuded self-confidence. Entering the room, he pulled out the chair directly across from Martin, sat, clasped his hands on the table, looked first at Pete then Martin in the eye, and asked, "How can I help?"

Based on Kurt's answers, it sounded like he and Carter worked for two different people. Kurt said he'd been learning the procedures and rules, thanks to Brooten, but Brooten was overbearing, nosy, and impossible to figure out. Brooten insisted on knowing his, Carter's, and Lauren's passwords, claiming it was company policy. "It's total BS," he said. "I have a friend who also works here, and his password is known only to him. Mr. Brooten claimed he had a responsibility to examine our work without giving us any advance notice, thereby keeping us on our toes and guaranteeing our work and emails were in keeping with company policies and protocols."

"Quite by accident," Kurt continued, "I discovered he'd changed the amounts I assigned for the payment of a claim. I didn't pull the amounts I designated out of thin air. I followed the guidelines established by Fundamentals to the letter, and I found no justifications for his changes. Regardless, why didn't he discuss it with me? Wasn't that his job? Had I not gone into the file to check on a detail, I'd never have known what he did.

The claim was processed with his changes, and I was listed as the claims adjuster. How dare he?" Kurt growled.

Good question, Pete thought and asked, "Did you discuss this with anyone?"

Kurt shook his head.

"Not even with your parents, siblings, or friends?"

"My parents have enough problems of their own, I don't have any siblings, and my friends spend so much tine complaining about their jobs, I have nothing to complain about in comparison. You're the only ones I've told. I looked for a long time, before landing this job. After I graduated, I discovered someone with a political science major wasn't exactly in demand. I'm afraid to bite the hand that feeds me. Don't want to end up on the street."

"What's your take on what Brooten did?" Martin asked.

"Sorry, but what I say might go beyond this room, and I can't risk it. Like I said, I need this job."

Pete asked, "How well did he get along with the other people around here and others present any time you were together?"

"I realize this may sound ungrateful or presumptuous, but I think he conned a lot of people around here. I don't think he's any prize. But to answer your question, he seemed to get along just fine. If he had enemies, I don't know who they were."

"Had he been acting different lately? Was he angry, testy, more distracted or nervous, anything like that?" Pete asked.

Kurt smiled and said, "He was always angry and testy, but I don't think he was any different."

Kurt took the bus to work, because it was cheaper than the cost for parking, and he couldn't depend on his silver 2001 Camry to get him back and forth without breaking down.

Pete then asked, "Got a cell in no way funded by your job?"

Kurt nodded.

Pete tore a page out of his notepad and pushed it toward Kurt. "Please write down the number. We may want to speak with you again."

Kurt did as requested and pushed the page back to Pete.

After looking at it, Pete said, "If I text or call, my name will not show. Instead, it will say, 'Blocked.' I understand you may not be able to answer or respond immediately, but please don't ignore a call or text."

"Fair enough. I know you have a job to do."

"What is your reaction to the news of his death?" Martin asked.

Kurt shrugged and said, "Don't know yet. Time will tell."

Pete and Martin thanked him, and he left to send in Brooten's third staff member. While they waited, both men wondered whether the third person's opinions would more closely resemble Kurt's or Carter's.

The next person who joined them was a tall, slender woman in her twenties with long black hair, large hazel eyes, and an inquisitive smile. She wore camel-colored wool slacks, a cream-colored silk blouse, and a brown wool blazer.

Stepping up to the table, she held out a hand to Martin, and said, "I'm Lauren Montgomery. Mr.

Hardwick said Mr. Brooten died this morning, and you want to talk to everyone he supervised. It seems crazy that he's gone. No guarantees in this life, huh?"

"Have a seat," Pete said after shaking her hand.

"What did you think of Fred Brooten as a supervisor?" he asked.

"I assume you're looking for the truth, not the politically correct answer."

"Definitely," Pete said.

"Wayne was one of the original three of Fred's trainees, along with Kurt and me, but he was fired because Mr. Brooten was afraid of him."

"Why was Brooten afraid of him?" Martin asked.

"Wayne was convinced he was on the take. He was gathering information to prove it, and Mr. Brooten found the emails with attached files Wayne sent himself. That's how Wayne discovered Mr. Brooten was checking every email we sent and not only checking our work but also digging into all the files on our computers. Wayne believed Mr. Brooten got a kickback from some of the claims he processed. Mr. Brooten took Wayne's ID, and he was escorted out the door. In other words, he was fired."

Lauren went on, "I had Wayne's phone number and called him at home that night. He told me what he believed, and about Mr. Brooten accessing our computers. He said for all he knew, the phones are tapped." She paused.

"Ever since he was fired, and it's been more than four months, Wayne hasn't been able to get a decent job. He believes it's because Fundamentals Insurance, namely Mr. Brooten, was providing extremely negative referrals, and he's now banned by the insurance industry. These days, he's working full time at the McDonald's on

Marion Street and University, and he drives for Uber nights and weekends to make ends meet."

Lauren looked down and said, "When I was young, I believed if you worked hard, did a good job, and kept your nose clean, you'd be successful."

Looking up again, she sighed and said, "Naive, huh?"

"Did you find anything peculiar with the way Brooten did business?" Pete asked. "Anything to support what Wayne said?"

Lauren shook her head and said, "But I've never seen any of the claims I processed, once I gave them to Mr. Brooten. So, if he changed anything, I'm not aware of it."

"I urged Wayne to send an anonymous letter to top management," she added. "I thought he might be able to get his job back and maybe even get some kind of bonus if he could prove he was right. He said he no longer has access to any of the incriminating information. I think he feels beaten." When it came to her experience with Brooten as her supervisor, Lauren said he was impatient and critical, but had no basis for comparison. This was her first job after college. The only Brooten enemies she could identify were Wayne and herself. She didn't believe Wayne would murder Fred, and she certainly hadn't.

Like Carter and Kurt, she'd seen no difference in the way Brooten acted in the recent past.

She had a white 2015 Corolla and said she drove to work, because it meant she could sleep until 7:00. If she took the bus, she'd have to get up thirty minutes earlier, and she admitted she was "not a morning person."

The two investigators learned Wayne's last name was Lewiston, got his phone number, and thanked Lauren for her help.

In hushed tones she told them, "I'm busy looking for a new job. Have a few leads. Wish me luck."

They did so, followed her out of the meeting room, and returned to Hardwick's office.

Joe sat at his desk, behind the mountain of paper that appeared to have grown since they left to meet with Brooten's staff. He took off his half-lens bifocals, rubbed his eyes, and asked, "Get what you needed?"

"We have a few additional questions," Pete said.

Hardwick frowned and asked, "Such as?"

"Tell us about Wayne Lewiston," Pete said.

"What about him?"

"Didn't Fred Brooten fire him?" Pete asked, wondering why the question needed clarification.

"Yes, he did, and with good reason."

"So you supported Fred Brooten's decision to do so?" Pete asked.

"Of course. Fred had no choice."

"Why is that?" Martin asked.

"Lewiston was in violation of our company policies."

"Did Lewiston discuss the matter with you?" Martin asked.

Joe let out a long, slow breath and said, "I don't remember. It's been several months."

"You didn't get Lewiston's side of the story?" Martin asked.

"Fred told me all I needed to know, and maybe you're right. Maybe Lewiston is the person who went after Fred."

"HR must have Lewiston's home address," Pete said. "Please get it for us."

"I doubt they still have it. His last check was automatically deposited to whatever account he gave us when we hired him. There was no need to hold onto his home address, once he was dismissed. Outdated information just clutters and complicates things."

"Actually, there was a reason to keep it in the system," Pete said. "The company had to send him his W-2 forms. So please call HR or accounting or whatever department handles those things and get his home address."

Hardwick rolled his eyes and reached for the phone. A minute later, he grabbed a pen and scrambled frantically through the litter on his desk, looking for a clean piece of paper. Eventually, he got the address, hung up, and handed Pete the full-sized sheet of paper with his barely legible scribbling sprawled across the page.

Pete glanced at it, making sure he could decipher it, them folded it and stuck it in a pocket.

"That's all for now," Pete said. "We'll be looking for your email."

Grumbling all the way, Hardwick escorted them back through cubicle city to the front door.

They thanked him for his cooperation, and he grunted, "Yeah."

Waiting for the elevator, Martin asked, "Next?"

FOURTEEN
Geraldine Mayer, Condo Association Member at Large

Before answering Martin's question about what was next on their agenda, Pete called the McDonald's on University Avenue. He learned that Wayne Lewiston got off at 3:15 today. Then he told Martin, "On the job front, speaking with Wayne Lewiston is, of course, a priority, but I think we'll be more successful if we show up at McDonald's just before he leaves. After speaking with him, we may get back to Kurt Worthington. What do you think about speaking with Brooten's neighbors and the other members of the board of directors of his condo association next?"

"Good idea, but what about lunch? I don't want to pass out."

"Can you stay conscious long enough to meet with one or two people, then take a break? By the way, have I told you recently how terrific you look since you lost all that weight, Martin? You do."

"Thanks. It's impossible to hear that too often. If necessary, I'll gnaw on my knuckles."

"Great. We have the phone numbers for the members of the board. Let's split them up and see what we can arrange. While at the condos, we can also check on the progress Forensics is making at Brooten's condo."

Martin took the vice-president and the secretary. Pete took the treasurer and the member at large. Between them, they reached, and then arranged a meeting with, the member at large at 1:45 and the secretary at 2:05. They left messages for the treasurer and vice president.

Geraldine Mayer, the member at large, was waiting for them when they arrived at the entrance to her building. She was an energetic, medium-sized octogenarian with green eyes and brown hair interspersed with threads of gray. She wore jeans, an embroidered navy sweatshirt, and buckskin Keds.

After they dispensed with the introductions, she said, "Follow me, please. I'm on the third floor. That insures I get plenty of exercise. Have to keep the ticker in good shape. I'm planning to stick around at least another twenty years. You boys look like you can climb a few flights, no sweat. Or should I say, 'No perspiration?'" She chuckled and took off up the first flight.

She's not even breathing heavy, Pete thought when they arrived at Geraldine's door.

Reaching in a front pocket of her jeans, she extracted a key fob that sported a bright-blue tag shaped like the State of Minnesota. "Courtesy of a grandson," she said, referring to the fob. "All nine of my grandkids are overly protective. I try to just smile and keep my opinions to myself. Don't want to hurt any of them."

Entering her condo, Pete and Martin found themselves in a beautifully decorated, compact living room. On their left were two sky-blue velvet chairs, separated by an end table. On their right was a quilted floral loveseat. A gallery of 8 X 10 photos with wood frames filled one wall.

Family, Pete thought.

"Have a seat," Geraldine said, motioning to the chairs, and I'll get you some coffee. I also made sandwiches, in case you haven't had time for lunch. Have you?" She smiled.

"Well, no, but we hate putting you out," Pete said.

"I'll be put out if they go to waste needlessly." She smiled and darted into the kitchen, returning with two plates. Each held a thick sandwich with homemade wheat bread, and oozing meat, cheese, tomato, and lettuce. Then she returned to the kitchen long enough to get napkins, a bowl with chips, and a plate with celery and carrots. "I like to cater to all tastes," she said, holding out the chips and veggies to Pete and Martin.

When both men took the veggies and passed on the chips, she said, "Health conscious, huh? Happy to see it. Thought that might be the case when I saw you. I guess you have to stay fit to chase your suspects through the streets, don't you."

"Fortunately, we don't have to do that very often," Martin said and smiled.

Geraldine left them long enough to get three mugs of coffee. After setting them on coasters on the end table she said, "Okay, I heard about Fred. How can I help?"

"First," Martin asked, "what does it mean to be a member at large on the board of directors?"

"It means I'm the tie-breaker." Geraldine beamed. "If the other four members, the ones with more impressive titles are in a standoff, I decide if the decision is yes or no, for or against."

"In other words," Pete said, "you're indispensable. Without you, nothing might ever get accomplished around here."

Geraldine gave him a thumbs up. "And that's what I tell them each time I ask for a raise."

"The members of the board are paid?" Pete asked.

"Well, no." Geraldine laughed.

"How about the board of directors?" Martin asked. "What do they do ... besides vote?" He smiled.

"We're the governing body and do things like hire people to maintain the buildings and grounds, enforce the rules and regulations, settle disputes among the residents, prepare an annual budget, and do long-term projections of future costs to determine the need for increases in the monthly assessments charged to the owners. The president takes the lead in those areas, and the VP is mostly their backup. Prior to hiring a management company, the treasurer collected and deposited our monthly assessments and paid the bills. Now the management company collects and deposits those fees. So, as best I can tell, the treasurer pays the bills, tracks our income and expenses, and keeps records of our account balances. The secretary takes minutes at the bimonthly board meetings."

"You were elected to the board?" Pete asked.

"Actually, I'm the last member who was elected, and that was almost four years ago. The association seems unable to get a quorum, permitting us to vote to fill the vacancies. So for the last three years, new board members have been appointed, not elected.

"The annual meetings are always on Mondays," Geraldine continued, "and I keep pushing to try a different day of the week. Maybe Mondays are bad for a lot of people. No luck. What would it hurt to try a different day?"

She added, "All terms are four years. Can't decide if I'll run again. It's almost impossible to find anyone willing to serve, so I'm sure I can stay on the board if I want to. The million dollar question is, do I want any more of this?

"Fred was president of the board?" Pete asked.

"Yes. The board votes for its officers. By the way, he volunteered to be on the board and was appointed, not elected."

"Was Fred a good president?" Martin asked.

"Depends on who you ask."

"What do you think?" Martin asked.

"I think he liked to throw money at every problem. I don't think we spent enough time researching the options."

"Let's start with the carpeting in the common areas," Geraldine continued. "Fred recommended cleaning all of it twice each year. I suggested buying higher-quality runners and shampooing as needed, based on a quarterly examination. The thing is, the people in some buildings are much messier than those in others. The board approved Fred's recommendation. ... Then there's the issue of when the common areas are painted. Fred recommended we do half of the buildings, so four, each year. I've lived here for going on twenty years. Prior to Fred, the common areas were never painted more often than every fifth year. A good scrubbing is often all that's needed. I mentioned those things, and Fred insisted a fresh coat of paint every second year is what his friend recommends for apartment complexes. As a rule, people move in and out of apartments much oftener than condominiums. Also, I think many apartment dwellers are more reckless about the way they treat those common areas. No pride of ownership."

"Again I recommended doing a regular assessment and painting when the board deems it necessary. Fred insisted he didn't have time to inspect all the buildings all the time, so I offered. I'm retired and would find a way to fit it into my jam packed schedule." Geraldine winked.

"Fred pressured the other members of the board to respect the recommendations of his so-called pro. And he won. In my opinion, he wins through coercion and intimidation." She was not smiling.

"Afterwards, I asked for the name of that pro. He refused to say and told me to stop being such a poor loser. Frankly, I wonder if that pro is a friend of his. I checked the job that the person we hired did in my building a year ago. The work looks like we went with the low bid. The amount we paid indicates that the opposite is true. The problem is, I've always been careful how I spend my money and, because these things are funded through the monthly assessments, it is my money." Geraldine frowned.

Pete asked, "Don't the members have to approve things like painting the common areas before they can happen?"

"Until Fred was the president, yes. He's convinced the board that the painting and lots of other remodeling and improvements are repairs, so that no longer happens."

"I could go on and on, but I'm sure you've got the idea. I feel sorry for his family, but as far as I'm concerned, Fred's death is no loss."

Geraldine thought the vice president and secretary of the board were likely to mourn Fred's passing. "He led them around like a herd of blind sheep," she said, "and they probably won't know what to do without him."

She was uncertain about the treasurer.

On the other hand, as best she knew, most of the other owners felt the way she did. "It might be at least partly my fault," she admitted. "Guess I should keep my mouth shut more." She blushed.

"Don't the owners have a right to know what's going on?" Pete asked.

"Yes, but did I tell them what was going on, or my read on what was going on?" She sighed.

"Are you aware of any owners who strongly disliked Fred?" Martin asked.

Geraldine smiled. "Are you asking me to provide a list of suspects?"

"No," Pete said. "We're looking for your help in making our list more complete and accurate."

"Sorry, I don't know anyone who hated him that much."

"Okay," Pete said, "who hated him, but not 'that much?'"

"Actually, I don't know of anyone who hated him. Saying they were unhappy with what he was doing, and how much it cost them, would be more accurate."

Pete and Martin thanked her for a delicious lunch and her time, gave her their business cards, and asked her to let them know if she came up with anything she thought might be useful.

On the way out of Geraldine's building, Pete said, "Do you think Geraldine saw you gnawing on your knuckles as we drove into the parking lot, interpreted it as a sign of starvation, and that's why she made lunch?"

"If so, I'm glad she's so perceptive." Martin chuckled. They had both devoured the lunch.

They left the car where Martin parked when they arrived and scrambled the length of the parking lot to get to their next meeting on time. On the way, they saw the FSU vehicle parked alongside the "No Parking Fire Lane" sign in front of Fred's building, indicating Forensics was still scouring the victim's condo.

Smiling, Pete gave Martin a thumbs up.

FIFTEEN
David Clements, Condo Association Secretary

David Clements was a handsome, middle-aged man of average height and build with strawberry-blond hair, blue eyes, and a smattering of freckles. He wore jeans, a frayed sweatshirt, and slippers. Although fully dressed and living on the first floor, he buzzed them in rather than coming to the entrance and opening the door. Apparently he trusted that no one but the men he expected had rung his doorbell.

Now familiar with the layout of these buildings, they went straight to his door. David stood in front of it, arms crossed, waiting. He too knew about Fred.

"Can you believe it?" he asked. "What the hell is going on that a guy can't even drive to work without being attacked? Where are you guys when we really need you? Passing out speeding tickets?"

"Well, sir, we do our best, but the budget doesn't permit us to provide private security for everyone living in St. Paul," Pete said calmly.

Martin, on the other hand, felt his body temperature rising.

"I suppose this could take a while, so you might as well come in and sit down," Clements said and grabbed a chair as he walked through his living room and into the small kitchen.

Clements placed the chair he carried at the table, which already had two chairs, and plopped into it.

Martin took the chair just inside the door.

Pete walked around the table and behind Clements to the other chair.

"Sorry I'm so angry," Clements said. "Things aren't going well at work, and now this. Losing Fred could be devastating to this place. What exactly happened to him?"

"Sorry, we aren't able to release that information at this time," Pete said. "All we can tell you is that he was attacked early this morning and died, and we have some questions that will help with our investigation."

"Such as?"

Pete began, "You served on the board of directors with Mr. Brooten, so you probably had an opportunity to see how the owners of these condominiums reacted to him."

"Yes. I think most of them appreciated how much he did to improve the appearance of the complex. He spent untold hours looking for ways to save money by finding the best deals on all kinds of essentials, such as keeping the trees trimmed so the lawn mowers could get under them and keeping the common areas looking neat and clean. Things like that."

"In your opinion, did he ever go overboard?" Martin asked.

"Who have you been talking to?" Clements fumed. "Fred was never recognized for his efforts, nor all his accomplishments. Until he came along, the board was sorely lacking in someone to take the bull by the horns. A complex like this doesn't run itself, and everything costs money."

"How long have you lived here?" Pete asked.

"Six years."

"What do you do for a living?" Pete asked.

"I sell real estate. Took it up after I bought this place and realized you make a lot more by selling a home than a TV, stereo, computer, washer, or dryer. Of course you don't sell as many, but the difference in the size of the commissions more than makes up for that. I now also have more control of my schedule. And I don't have to push for the purchase of inferior products with a greater markup. I hated lying to customers in order to maximize my commission."

"Can I have one of your business cards?" Pete asked. "We aren't yet ready to start looking, but our family is growing, and one of these days my wife and I will have to start looking for a larger home," Pete fibbed, trying to get David to warm up and relax.

David jumped up, took off down the hall, and returned with a stack of business cards. He handed them all to Pete, smiled, and said, "Please share them with your family and friends."

Squelching a smile, Martin asked, "When you began selling real estate, I suppose you had to buy a fancy new car."

"Yeah. That was the big drawback, but appearances are everything ... after location, of course." He chuckled.

"What do you drive?" Martin asked.

"A 2010 Lexus LX. Managed to save a few bucks by buying an immaculate used car."

"Does color also matter?" Martin asked.

"Well, black is too nondescript and magnifies the dirt, so mine is gold."

"Did you socialize with Fred?" Pete asked.

"No, I considered Fred a friend, but I don't think he had time to socialize. And my social circle is pretty well limited to family and a handful of high school and college friends."

"Any idea who might have wanted to hurt Fred?" Pete asked.

"Unfortunately, lots of the people who live here. Specifically those who place their bank balances ahead of the appearance of their homes. I got rid of my house when I decided I didn't want to invest the amount of time required to maintain it. Decided to move to a place where I didn't have to shovel or mow the lawn, find a painter or a roofer, right on down the line. Unfortunately, too many of the owners wanted that as well, but thought in the process they were also eliminating the costs. How dumb is that?"

"How about some names? We won't assume anything, but you could help us find a starting point." Martin said.

David shook his head. "As a member of the board, I'm not in a position to name any names."

"How about as a friend to Fred?" Martin asked.

"This will take some thought. How about if I get back to you tomorrow?"

Pete and Martin stood and went through the usual routine. They thanked David for his time, gave him their business cards, and said they'd appreciate his help in determining who did something so unthinkable.

"Both ends of the spectrum," Martin said as they walked out of David's building and headed to Forensics.

Sixteen
Forensics

Crossing the lot to Fred's building, Pete called the central line for Forensics and asked to be connected with the team assigned to the condo of victim Frederick Brooten. In no time at all, he reached an investigator currently in Fred's condo. That investigator, Roy, reached the entrance right after they did and let them in.

To avoid being overheard, Pete and Martin stuck with small talk until they were inside Brooten's condo, and the door was closed behind them.

This was their first time in this condo, and Pete and Martin checked it out, amazed at the hovel Brooten had called home. Dirty dishes on the table was reasonable for someone who rushed out the door around 5:00 a.m., but that didn't explain the fast-food containers and dishes on the counters and in the sink. Here was a guy who insisted on painting the common areas every two years, and his walls were in dire need of a washing and/or a coat of paint. Dust balls were abundant on the hardwood floors, and a thick layer of dust covered every flat surface. The windows were so dirty that they muted the outdoor light, and about three times the optimum amount of furniture for the available space crowded each room.

FSU investigators were in every room, examining every drawer and closet, looking over and under every surface. They worked to uncover any clues about the man who died this morning on Jackson.

Observing all of this, Pete asked Roy, "Finding anything?"

Roy smiled and said, "We assumed we'd need a search warrant to obtain his banking information, once we determined the bank. These days, almost everyone does their banking electronically. Mr. Brooten was an exception.

"We found a file cabinet squashed into the second bedroom, which he used as a den. It's piled high with magazines and books that look like they've never been opened. His credit union statements and taxes for the last ten years are jammed into it. The balance in his checking account was always a few hundred dollars. The balance in his savings account was low double digits. Per his taxes, he either does all of his banking with the credit union or the balances are so low he hasn't earned $10 in interest in a year from any other account. There is no record of any stocks or bonds in his taxes or anywhere in the filing cabinet.

"Found his mortgage for this place. He paid ten percent down. Sold a house a month later, but owed almost as much as the buyer paid. After closing costs, he walked away with enough to buy a cup of coffee, as long as he didn't get it at Starbucks.

"His take-home pay, if he is paying child support," Roy continued, "is almost consumed by his payments for this condo and his credit card minimum monthly payments."

"How about payments for his truck?" Pete asked. "He drove a GMC Sierra. Where was he getting the money for those payments, and how did he manage to get approved for that loan? He couldn't have paid cash for it, could he?"

"We found the paperwork for the truck. He purchased it from a used-car dealer. The bill of sale says the final price was $80,200, and he paid $5,200 down. If he financed that purchase through a bank or his credit union, that paperwork should be with the bill of sale. And there should be payments showing up somewhere.

"The only payments appearing on his credit union statements are the mortgage for this condo, which includes the principle, interest, taxes, and insurance. Then there are those for the condo association fees, those for his cellphone and electric bills, and always for the minimum due to his credit card companies. Wondered how he was paying for the truck, until Terry found a metal box under his bed." Roy smiled.

"And?" Pete asked.

"The box appeared to have been hidden behind some storage boxes under his bed."

"And?" Martin asked.

"The box contains $63,250, mostly in hundred-dollar bills. Any gambling winnings, including from casinos and the lottery have to be reported on your 1040. Lots of people are negligent, but anytime you win more than something like $2,500, the casino, lottery, pull tabs seller, or whomever must issue a W2G to you and provide a copy to the IRS. In the last ten years, Brooten hasn't claimed a penny of gambling winnings or losses on his taxes. And there is no paper trail showing the source of these funds."

"Sports betting with someone off the grid?" Pete asked.

"Possible, I guess, but that's a lot of dough."

"We've been interviewing the people on the board of directors for this complex, as well as the people who reported to him at his place of employment," Pete told Roy. "More than one suggested he was on the take. That could explain the cash. If people were paying him for cooking the books or illegitimately sending business their way, it would be crazy to leave a paper trail. Don't you agree?"

"Absolutely."

"So," Pete continued, "they almost had to deal in cash. We hope to meet with a person we've been told believed that about him this afternoon, as well as the other members of the board and some residents. One of the people he supervised said a coworker was gathering information to prove what was happening, and Brooten found out what he was doing. He was fired immediately. Apparently he no longer has access to any of the data, but I wonder what he'd found."

"Keep us in the loop," Roy said.

"Absolutely. If what we heard is true, we may need your help in checking out some of the people or companies suspected of participating in Fred's schemes."

Pete and Martin got the name of the used-car lot that sold the truck to Brooten. They'd find out how he was making the payments. Could he be paying cash? Why? Wouldn't it be easier and more economical to deposit all that cash and write a check? Where did he get it, who was he hiding it from, and why?

They thanked the FSU investigators and left Brooten's condo. Reaching the building entrance, Pete checked his phone and said, "No response to the message I left for the treasurer. Have you heard from the VP?"

Martin checked and shook his head.

"In that case, can we make it to the used-car lot and back to McDonald's by 3:10?"

"Heck yes," Martin said optimistically.

They ran to the unmarked car, anxious to learn how Brooten bought an $80,000 truck.

SEVENTEEN
Oaks Used Cars

With a goal of reaching McDonald's no later than 3:10 to keep Lewiston from skipping out on them, they headed north and east to Oaks Used Cars on Highway 61.

Pete made good use of the travel time by researching Fundamentals on the way. In the process, he learned it was a publicly traded company. He also found a list of the top executives and wrote them in his notepad. "This will come in handy, if Hardwick decides not to cooperate," he told Martin.

"You aren't really anticipating he'll come across with the information you requested, are you, Pete?"

Pete laughed and said, "No, but think how much time we'll save if he does."

Martin pulled into the Oaks parking lot, and a salesperson wearing a broad smile reached them before Martin turned off the car. "Whatever you're looking for," he said, "we've got it at a price you'll like."

"Actually," Martin said, "we're looking for information about a car you sold in December. It's a red GMC Sierra. Remember that truck?"

"Did a big guy buy it? There aren't any problems, are there?"

The two investigators pulled out their badges and IDs and showed them to him.

"Whoa! If you're suggesting we did something illegal, we didn't. We would never consider anything like that."

"We have no reason to doubt that," Pete said. "What we want to know is how he paid for it. Haven't found any record of a loan."

"He came in regularly, always looking for something bigger and better than the truck he was driving. One day, he showed up just after we bought the Safari from a guy who couldn't keep up the payments and was about to lose it. We managed to work a sweet deal with that man, and hours later worked a sweet deal with ..." He paused, snapped his fingers and said, "Fred, right?"

The two investigators nodded.

"Yeah, I remember him." The salesperson smiled. "Let's talk about it inside, so I can stop shivering."

He led them the length of the lot, hoping to tempt them with at least one of the bargains on display, then ushered them inside to his desk and offered them coffee.

Both men declined, wanting only to get some answers and head to McDonald's.

"Fred is hard to forget, in part due to his size," the salesperson said. "He wanted that truck in the worst way, but said he wouldn't qualify for a loan. He spent about two hours trying to work out a payment method. Some of his suggestions were laughable. Finally, he said if we'd work with him, he'd bring in $5,000 in cash by the tenth of every month for eighteen months. We aren't a bank and we don't finance vehicles, but that way he'd pay significantly more than we had, and it was the only way he could buy it. Besides, if he missed a payment, the truck would come right back here." His smile broadened.

Neither Pete nor Martin told him that the Sierra would probably be back in their lot before long.

They thanked him and turned to walk to Martin's car, but the salesperson stopped them. "Before you go, take my business card," he said, handing one to each of them. "I'm sure you know, the biggest loss in a new car's value happens when you drive it off the lot. You save a substantial sum by buying a used car. I'm Allen Dexter. Look me up the next time you're in the market. I'll better the best deal you can get anywhere else."

They tucked the cards in their pockets and headed for McDonald's. On the way, Pete told Martin, "I wonder how legit it is to charge $15,000 in interest on a loan of $75,000 for a period of eighteen months."

Martin shook his head and said, "Yeah, and how did they figure Fred could legitimately come up with $5,000 in cash for eighteen months and not qualify for a loan."

"Good point."

On the way to their next meeting, Pete contacted headquarters and recruited assistance in getting Wayne Lewiston's driver's license photo. It could come in handy, or even be critical, when they reached Lewiston's location. It arrived, via a text, while they were still en route.

Thanks to Martin's heavy foot, they reached McDonald's a few minutes ahead of Pete's targeted arrival time and parked in the lot on the south side of the building. This McDonald's looked more like a bank than a fast-food place. Perhaps that was because, in a previous life, it was a bank. On a bright, cloud-free early morning, the Minnesota State Capitol fell only a bit short of casting a shadow over this McDonald's.

EIGHTEEN
Wayne Lewiston, Fundamentals Insurance

The two investigators split up. Pete walked into McDonald's and got into one of the lines of people waiting to place their orders. Standing there, he carefully monitored both exits.

Martin positioned himself outside and on the western side of the southwest corner. From that location, he had an unobstructed view of anyone going out the back door—presumably the employee entrance—without being seen. Martin and Pete had both memorized Wayne Lewiston's driver's license photo. They'd recognize him.

Knowing he might be there for a bit, Martin decided to multitask. He called the ME's office to check on the schedule for Brooten's autopsy. Learned it would be at 4:30 that afternoon.

Since that took little time, he called Forensics for an update on the crime scene investigation. Before the investigator got into it, Martin explained he might have to disconnect without warning. Said he was on a stakeout, of sorts, and smiled.

Forensics was still scouring the area where the body was found. Thus far, the only thing they'd found in the way of trace evidence was some navy fibers off a scarf or stocking cap in the underbrush outside the northwest edge of the Troutbrook parking lot. The person who shot Brooten might have used the underbrush to camouflage their presence from anyone traveling south on Jackson, namely Brooten. On the other hand, they could have been left there by any visitor to the sanctuary ... or anyone passing through.

Thus far, they had no evidence that the person who shot Brooten escaped by following the trail, but they couldn't rule it out. It seemed more likely the person parked along "old" Maryland for a quick and easy getaway. Since the two businesses facing the Troutbrook parking lot are closed until mid- to late-afternoon, and the location of the shooting wasn't visible to any of the homes on the south side of Jackson and Maryland, there was little danger of being seen while going to and from that location. However, they hadn't found any trace evidence supporting that possibility.

The line Pete waited in moved quickly, and he used the opportunity to check out and eliminate all the employees visible from his location. His overcoat hid his Glock from everyone, and he hoped that improved his and Martin's chances of conferring with Lewiston.

As he reached the front of the line, Pete saw Lewiston move from the back, possibly where the drive-through was located, and approach an employee at the far end of the counter.

He told the woman who asked for his order that he needed to speak with Wayne Lewiston and nodded in Wayne's direction.

She walked over to Wayne and said, "He wants to talk to you," and tilted her head toward Pete.

Wayne looked puzzled, but stepped over to Pete.

Pete stepped to his right, so he didn't hold up the line, and Lewiston followed his lead.

"We need to talk," Pete said. "I'm a police officer, and I need your help."

Wayne looked at him out of the corner of his eye and said, "I don't understand, and I can't talk now. I'm working."

"A few hours ago, my partner and I spoke with Lauren Montgomery about Fred Brooten. She was very helpful. Based on what she said, you could be as or more helpful. It's important we speak with you. It won't take long, and we're willing to wait until you're finished working. When will that be?"

"Shortly, but I need to get right home."

"Like I said, it won't take long, and if you need a ride, we'll drop you off." Thanks to Hardwick, Pete had Lewiston's address. It was so close, he figured Lewiston probably walked to work. Hoping it would provide an incentive, he added, "The questions are regarding Fred Brooten. Perhaps we can help. No promises, but there's a chance."

"How?" Lewiston asked, showing an interest for the first time.

"Let's talk about it as soon as you get off."

Lewiston sighed and said, "Fine. Hang tight." Then he disappeared behind the counter.

Pete texted Martin, saying he'd spoken with Lewiston, but to stay put.

"We need some privacy," Pete said a few minutes later, when Lewiston reappeared. "You can recommend a place, or we can."

"Can we talk in your car?"

Pete rejected that suggestion. He and Martin had to be able to see and read Lewiston's facial expressions.

"How about if my partner and I get you a Coke or coffee or something to eat somewhere? We could also take you to our office and show you around if you'd like to see it."

"Why don't we just go to my place?"

"Where do you live?" Pete asked, not wanting to raise Lewiston's suspicions.

"In an apartment just off Rice and south of Como."

Pete hurriedly sent a text to Martin, saying, "Meet U at car," then delayed his and Lewiston's arrival there by leading Lewiston out the wrong door. On the way he said, "My partner is waiting for us in the lot."

Martin got the address from Lewiston, and they drove to his apartment. Wayne wanted to get as many questions as possible out of the way before they arrived. But Pete and Martin foiled that plan by asking about his family and friends, hometown, and where he went to school. In the process, they learned a lot about him, including the fact he didn't own a car.

The apartment was compact, and the furnishings were sparse, but everything looked neat and clean.

While getting them situated in the living room, Wayne explained, "I'm just getting started and intent on living within my means. Now that I'm working at McDonald's and for Uber, those means are far more meager than I'd anticipated. You said you spoke with Lauren. She probably told you what happened." He blushed.

"She mentioned it, Pete said, "but let me back up a minute. You should know that Fred Brooten was attacked this morning and died ..."

Wayne's eyes went wide as he fell back in his chair, held up his hands, palms out, and said, "You don't think I did that, do you? I didn't!" he shouted, shaking his head wildly.

Rather than answering that question, Martin said, "We're here because, based on your dealings with him, we think you might be able to help us determine who did."

Wayne shook his head feverishly and said, "I have no idea who did it."

"We want to talk to you about his work practices," Pete explained. "It's possible his death has something to do with them. For example, you questioned some of the things he did?"

"Yeah, and that got me promoted to a job at McDonald's."

"Have you changed your mind about your conclusions?" Martin asked.

"Not a chance! But I've been wondering if I handled it the wrong way."

"Tell us what you found and how," Pete said.

"Well, after what I would call an unacceptably brief orientation, Brooten assigned Carter, Lauren, and me several claims that we were supposed to handle on our own, then turn over the paperwork to him. While doing this, I researched several cases similar to mine, including the items that were and were not covered, went over the policies with a fine-tooth comb to make sure everything I approved was covered, and getting actual costs in order to determine the reimbursement amounts. Then I negotiated the settlements with the company representatives. By the time I'd finished, I was confident I'd done a good and accurate job of processing each claim, and I forwarded them to Brooten. He insisted we call him Mr. Brooten or sir, not Fred. It seemed the authority went straight to his head, but whatever. It didn't matter to me."

Wayne went on, "Hearing nothing from him in the way of challenges, criticisms, suggestions or praise, I continued processing claims in the same manner, assuming I was doing a good job. And why would he permit me to negotiate settlements if he wasn't confident I knew what I was doing?

"Brooten, Lauren, Carter, and I got together one afternoon in a meeting room, and he asked me to get some forms off his desk. While looking for them, I saw two cover sheets for claims I'd settled. The settlements weren't for the amounts I'd negotiated. I had to know where I'd messed up, so I scanned one of them. By then, I was so familiar with the forms, I knew right where to look. I could see that Brooten had increased the amount reimbursed on some items and approved an item I'd determined was ineligible. My jaw dropped. I'd carefully researched those things, and I was pretty sure I was right in all cases.

"While scanning the second settlement, I heard someone breathing deeply and headed toward Brooten's office. I always knew when he was approaching my cube, because he breathed like he'd smoked a carton of cigarettes every day of his life. So I grabbed the forms he'd asked for and sped out of his office. I don't know who'd been out there, but there was no one around when I left his office."

Shaking his head, Wayne continued, "Well, I waited a couple of weeks, thinking he'd say something about those changes. He never did, so I met with him one day, which became my last day with the company, to discuss his modifications. He asked me how I dared to question his determinations. He said that, compared to him, I knew nothing. I tried to explain why I thought he was wrong, and he asked how I knew about the changes. I shut up. The next thing I knew, two security guards came to my cube, gave me five minutes to pack up my personal stuff, took my ID, and escorted me out the front door. And that's the end of my career with Fundamentals." Wayne frowned, sighed and shook his head.

"Did you make a note of the difference between Brooten's settlements and yours?" Pete asked.

"Yes, sir, and I still remember. The one I was able to scan through was for an additional $28,412. The second was for an additional $33,626."

"How can you remember seemingly random numbers like that?" Martin asked. "I'd understand if they were a series, but even so ..."

"Well, I have this thing for numbers. For example, I can recite my two credit card numbers, and the number on my driver's license. And of course I know my social security number."

"Why would Brooten modify your work?" Pete asked.

"It only makes sense to me if there was a benefit to either Fundamentals or Mr. Brooten himself. And I'd be shocked if he'd do it unless he himself benefited somehow. How could he? I can only surmise."

"Please do," Pete said.

"If he was fraudulently handling claims to improve the bottom line for Fundamentals Insurance, that seems pretty complicated. How would he benefit, unless someone at the top knew about it and was finding a way to reward him. It could be far more beneficial to him and far less complicated if he was the only player within Fundamentals Insurance."

Wayne continued, "He may have been able to work a deal with the claimant with whom he negotiated the settlements to overstate the losses and split the overage. It seems to me that would work only if those representatives were owners or in some way benefiting personally from the fraud Brooten was, I believe, perpetrating. The cases I discovered were both small companies, and the person with whom I'd negotiated was the owner. I, of course, have no idea what was happening with the claims Mr. Brooten himself settled nor the ones settled by Lauren and Carter.

"The thing is," Wayne continued, "why would he risk it? Why did he assign claims to us that there was a chance he'd change? It makes no sense to me. Granted he never discussed any changes with us, and it was coincidental that I discovered what he'd done with two of my settlements, but ... Do you suppose he was that arrogant? Or was he just reckless that particular day?"

"It seems foolish, but I've heard of crazier things," Pete said. "And sometimes people in a position of authority get arrogant. That's the good news, because sometimes that's the only reason their crimes are discovered."

"What are the names of the companies where you discovered the discrepancies?" Martin asked.

"If I tell you, will I be sticking my neck on a chopping block?" Wayne bit his lower lip.

"Well, Wayne, you're not the one in danger here," Martin said.

"But say Fred got greedy and one of those owners killed him. What's to keep them from coming after me next?"

"Your name wouldn't come up until after they were charged and jailed," Martin said. "If they were released, we'd provide protection to a valuable witness like you."

Relaxing, Wayne asked, "Can that protection be in the form of an attractive woman? You see, I'm an equal rights proponent." He grinned.

"We'd see what we could do," Martin chuckled.

After a few additional assurances, Wayne said, "They are the Horizon Laundry and the BPC Pet Hospital. BPC stands for Bark, Purr, Chirp. Crazy huh?"

"We understand you spoke with Lauren about this," Martin said. "Did you discuss it with anyone else?"

"When Mr. Brooten brushed me off, I tried to talk to Mr. Hardwick. He didn't want to hear anything I said. He told me I reported to Mr. Brooten, and I should discuss any job-related issues with him. I told him I'd tried, and he repeated that directive."

Martin asked, "Did you have a chance to observe Brooten's interactions with other employees at Fundamentals?"

"Occasionally, but mostly just the people like me who worked for him."

"How did people, other than your group, typically react to him?" Martin asked.

"He seemed to get along fine, but they were all his superiors, and I think he was Mr. Suck Up."

"You've been very helpful," Pete said. "We greatly appreciate your time and the information you've shared."

"Ditto," Martin said.

"Depending on how this plays out," Pete added, "we may need to get back to you."

Wayne nodded.

Before leaving, they gave him their business cards and asked him to call if he thought of anything else about the cases Brooten modified, or anyone else who might have had issues with or might have wanted to attack him.

Walking back to the unmarked car, Martin said, "If Wayne is right about Brooten, how can Fundamentals Insurance have such a wonderful opinion of him?"

"Wayne said he snowed a lot of people. He could be right."

Martin told Pete the time for the autopsy, and shared what he'd learned from Forensics.

Neither had heard from the other board member they'd contacted, so Pete said, "We don't have much time before the autopsy, but let's go back to Brooten's condo complex and speak with some of his neighbors. If Geraldine Mayer is right about the attitudes of the board members, speaking with the owners could be more productive."

On the way, he smiled and said, "I'll call Kathy Wheaton, the neighbor we spoke with first thing this morning, when trying to find Brooten's family. If she's home, she could be a good starting point. People her age often feel they've earned the right to state their opinions."

NINETEEN
Kathy Wheaton, Neighbor

Pete gave Martin a thumbs up when Kathy Wheaton picked up the phone on the second ring and said, "My phone says blocked, are you the police who were here at daybreak?"

As she descended the stairs, it was obvious Kathy hadn't slowed down since the last time they saw her. Opening the door, she invited them in and said, "Follow me and speak softly while we're in the hallways. These buildings are poorly insulated. You can hear everything anyone says when they talk in the halls."

After ushering them into her living room and pouring a mug of coffee for each of them, she pulled her chair in close and asked, "What happened to Fred?" She wore a smile, so both investigators had a good idea to which group she belonged.

Despite that, Pete began by asking, "Was he a friend of yours?"

"I could pick him out in a lineup, but I don't know anything about him, other than that by all indications he lives alone. I've never seen anyone except other members of our board of directors approach his door. Keep in mind, unless I'm coming or going, I don't see anyone in the hallways, and other than a biweekly trip to the grocery store and a weekly trip to the mailbox, about the only time I get out is for an occasional lunch with friends."

"Often the people who stick closest to home are the best informed, thanks to their networks," Pete said. "From your perspective, Kathy, did Fred have many enemies?"

"Good job, Detective. I love the way you baited the hook and cast, and are waiting to reel me in. You remind me of Danny on *Blue Bloods*."

"And what would you tell Danny, or my partner and me?"

"Well, my network doesn't deal in this type of information."

"So no one around here ever got angry with him or complained about him?"

"There was plenty of both, but none of the people here would kill him for that reason. Slash his tires? Maybe. Murder? No."

"Who would have liked to slash his tires?" Martin asked.

"That was just a figure of speech. Lots of the owners, in fact most of the owners, are unhappy about the hikes in the monthly association fees. Some are worried that at the current rate, soon they won't be able to afford to live here any longer. I'm one of them. The increases have been occurring at a record rate, and neither the grounds nor the buildings have improved one iota. In fact, many of us believe the quality of life is deteriorating."

"How so?" Martin asked.

"The board has had many trees trimmed to the point where they are no longer beautiful and no longer provide a measure of privacy. Things like that. I know it's a matter of taste, but all of those actions are costing us."

"Do you ever attend the board meetings?" Pete asked.

"I did a couple of times, but they couldn't be more sterile. The board doesn't discuss anything important until those of us not on the board are sent packing. They call it maintaining the privacy of the owners or something equally ludicrous."

"Have you ever thought about running for a seat on the board?" Pete asked.

"I was on the board for six years, and things went well. The buildings were well maintained, and we stayed within the budget. The current board seems to believe money is the solution to every problem. If they are spending money like drunken sailors, I don't care that only a small percentage of everything they spend comes out of my pocket. That doesn't make it logical or good business sense."

"What did you think of Fred as a person?" Pete asked.

"Like I told you, I'd recognize him in a police lineup, because of his size, unless another four or five people in the lineup were also huge. But I don't know him. I've never spoken with him."

"As the president of your association, he never took the time to introduce himself to all the owners?" Pete asked.

"Only at attempted annual meetings. We haven't had an annual meeting in years, because we can never get a quorum. Anyway, at those times, he stands up and tells us how wonderful he is. I'd love to lob some rotten tomatoes at him, but those meetings never happen during the summer months." Kathy chuckled.

"Anyone here you think we should be sure to interview?" Martin asked. "Someone who is generally in the know about what's going on?"

"I can only think of one person. That's Bernice Bethel. She's the person who always knows when the mail is delivered, FedEx, UPS, or Amazon has dropped off a package, things like that. She's the all-seeing all-knowing and may be able to help you."

Pete and Martin thanked Kathy, gave her their business cards, and asked her to notify them if she or her friends thought of anyone they should speak with and/or consider.

In closing, Pete said, "If you provide any names, Kathy, you're not accusing anyone of anything. You're just steering us in the direction that could help us solve this case."

TWENTY
The Autopsy

Tight on time, the two investigators ran from Kathy's apartment to the unmarked car. The autopsy was scheduled to begin in ten minutes.

"Will you attend the autopsy, Martin, or do you want me to cover it?" Pete asked as Martin settled in behind the steering wheel and started the car.

"I think I hear some paperwork at headquarters calling my name."

Pete laughed and asked, "Is it a nagging voice or just demanding?"

"Nagging. Definitely nagging."

Martin breathed a sigh of relief when he reached the ME's office. He was glad Pete was back for a lot of reasons, and his ability to skip this part of an investigation was one of them. That gave him an idea. "What's on our agenda after the autopsy, Pete?"

"We need to talk to the other two members of the board, and I'd like to speak with some owners who aren't on the board. Both men checked their phones. Neither had heard from the board member for whom they left a message, nor had they received an email from Joe Hardwick at Fundamentals Insurance.

"In other words, plenty to do but no fixed schedule, right?"

"Right."

"Well, I have an idea that I think will make your day and mine. How about if I call Katie to see if we can join her for dinner? Maybe we can pick up something, since I doubt she made enough for all of us."

"That's a great idea, Martin. We usually eat about 7:00, so she may still be considering the options and could be hoping to hear from me. Please call her and ask if it's okay if we stop on the way and pick up some steaks. Would that work for you?"

"That sounds fantastic." Martin smiled.

"If Katie doesn't like the idea of steaks, please ask her what she'd like us to get. Gotta go. Pick me up in two hours, unless I text a different time," Pete said and hustled into the Ramsey County ME's office, located just outside Regions Hospital.

The crew was happy to see him, and they had all kinds of questions about Katie and the baby for the proud dad. He answered all of them and added a few anecdotes that showed how much he enjoyed being a dad. He didn't mention that he was still grappling with whether he would remain an investigator.

Martin was waiting outside at the designated time, and Pete shared the results with him. "Frederick Brooten was a big man. More specifically, he was six foot two and 297 pounds. It seems the murderer was a marksman or took a lucky shot. Actually, it was an unlucky shot for Brooten, and due to the outcome, once caught, it will be for the shooter as well. He was shot in the neck at close range, and the bullet severed his brain stem, killing him instantly. So Don was right, when we spoke with him at the crime scene. The bullet then lodged in his spinal cord."

Pete continued, "The trajectory is curious. Since it appears Brooten was lunging forward when he was shot, the shooter had to be sitting or lying on the ground. Seems like a curious scenario, don't you agree, Martin?"

"Yeah." Martin agreed. "I can paint a few pictures of how it might have played out, but none of them make any sense to me."

"The bullet fragments are on their way to Forensics and, of course, will be analyzed and checked with the National Crime Information Center for any matches showing a record of the weapon being used in any previous crimes."

"If it was," Martin said, "that could make our job much easier ... or not. After all that, can you even think about food?" he added.

"Will be able to by the time we get to my place. What does Katie want us to pick up?"

Martin said, "She was pleased and said steaks would be fine. Asked you to call and let her know when to fire up the grill."

Pete called home and said they'd be there in about twenty minutes. That left enough time for him to run into a grocery store and pick up three rib eyes.

TWENTY-ONE
Martin Invites Himself to Dinner

Katie had been watching out the picture window, and she, Teddy, and Benji were waiting at the door when Pete and Martin walked in.

Benji jumped up and down, greeting Pete and Martin. Pete squatted down and scratched Benji behind his ears.

Then Pete hugged Katie, handed the steaks to Martin, and Katie passed him his son.

Smiling down at the baby, Pete said, "Did you hear what he just said? He asked how my day is going."

"I'm not surprised," said Katie. "He's spent the last thirteen hours asking when you'd be home and saying he hoped you wouldn't be too tired to play."

"And he probably read *The Iliad* and *The Odyssey* between naps." Martin laughed.

"No, Katie decided to save those until after his two-month birthday. Didn't you say he's reading something light, like *Aesop's Fables*, Katie?"

Katie shook her head and asked, "How long can you stay?"

"I figure an hour," Pete said. "Interviewing several people we've been unable to reach is a priority. They might have jobs. We have their addresses. If we don't hear from them in the next hour, I think we should show up at their doorsteps."

"So, how does playing with Teddy, then rocking him to sleep, while I finish the salad and grill the steaks sound to you, Pete?"

"You won't mind? That sounds unfair to you."

Katie laughed, rolled her eyes, and said, "I'm ready for a break. Both Teddy and I will love it."

"I'll be glad to help Katie," Martin said. "And I can make sure she doesn't burn the steaks." He laughed.

And that's the way they worked it.

Katie knew from experience that it took about fifteen minutes for Pete to put Teddy to sleep, so she gave him a heads-up when it was time to begin.

While Pete was busy with Teddy, Benji kept Katie and Martin company as they talked about Pete's first case since coming off paternity leave.

"He seems really happy," Martin said. "Do you mind that I suggested we come here for dinner, hoping he'll see there's a way to make being a dad and an investigator compatible?"

"Clever, Martin. Very clever, and thank you. It's so nice seeing you. I really miss talking to adults."

The grill was ready, so Katie and Martin put on their coats to go out on the deck and grill the steaks. As she opened the sliding-glass door, Martin heard Pete start singing Teddy to sleep.

"He has a nice voice," Martin said.

Katie grinned and said, "I'm thinking about recording it for bedtimes when he isn't home."

She was taking the steaks off the grill when Pete joined and asked, "What can I do?"

"Enjoy dinner," Katie said.

She'd already set the table, and she added the steaks, while Pete got the salad out of the refrigerator, and Martin poured the herbal tea he selected.

Over dinner, Martin updated Katie on his wife, Michelle, and their kids, Marty and Olivia. "They're growing so fast," he said. "Before you know it, Marty is going to want a car. Do you have any idea how much car insurance costs for a teenage boy? There goes the budget. I'm going to have to get a second job."

"With the hours we work, that'll be quite a trick." Pete laughed.

At least he's laughing about it, Martin thought optimistically.

Katie asked how it was going with their new case.

"Wrapped it up around noon," Pete said. "Aside from having to go to the autopsy, we spent the afternoon hunched over a pool table. Still having trouble with some bank shots, but practice, practice, practice."

"Your tenacity is what first attracted me to you, Pete," Katie deadpanned. "Then you were kidding about only having an hour for dinner, weren't you?"

Struggling to keep from smiling, Martin said, "Actually, no. We promised to take Commander Lincoln's grandkids to the arcade. You never know when some brownie points will come in handy."

Then he and Pete spent a few minutes sharing what information they could with Katie, before checking their phones for voice messages, texts, or emails from the people they were waiting on. It was unanimous. Nothing from anyone. So both called the board member they were waiting to hear from. And both calls were answered.

The VP told Martin she'd be free for the rest of the evening in around a half hour. The treasurer told Pete he was shopping and would be home in about an hour.

Sticking with Pete's original schedule, they left intent on meeting with another owner or two while waiting on the board members. After all, unless they wanted to start throwing their weight around, there was little else they could do in a case like this. And in a case like this, there was more to be lost than gained by throwing their weight around.

TWENTY-TWO
Other Condo Owners

Reaching the condo complex, Pete and Martin discovered that Forensics had departed. That wasn't surprising. After all, how long does it take to scour 1,000 square feet?

They decided to start with Brooten's building, since several units had lights on. It took four attempts before someone answered. That was Tim Scanlon. He lived on the third floor.

Learning who they were, Tim came down to let them in. He wore khakis, a light-blue Oxford-cloth shirt, a navy crewneck sweater, and slippers.

He was six feet tall, and showed no signs of a middle-age paunch. His thick, medium-brown hair was gray only at the temples. Pete estimated him to be in his late fifties or early sixties, thought he looked familiar, and tried to place him.

After leading them up the stairs to his condo, he told Pete and Martin he'd be surprised if anyone who lived in the complex hadn't heard about Brooten's death. He'd been told by at least four people.

Scanlon set the tone when he said he neither knew nor cared where Brooten worked or what he did for a living. Likewise, he knew nothing about Brooten's family or friends.

When asked what he did know about Brooten, Scanlon said, "I know he thinks president of the association and king are synonymous."

"You're not an admirer?" Martin asked.

"Believe me, no one admires Fred as much as the guy who looks back at him when he stands in front of a mirror."

"How well do you know him?" Martin continued.

"Almost everything I know about him is through meetings and correspondence. I've had no personal dealings with him, and I haven't spoken to him other than to say 'hi' when our paths cross."

"Why is that?" Martin continued.

"From all I've seen, he's a pompous ass, and I refuse to waste time with people like that. Life is too short. With rare exceptions, that's the overwhelming opinion."

"It sounds like Mr. Brooten doesn't have many friends around here. How about enemies?" Pete asked.

"Are you asking if anyone around here would kill him?" Tim smiled.

"Or want to kill him?" Pete added.

"I know a lot of people who wish he'd take a long walk off a short pier. Can't imagine any of them finding the initiative to do anything. And yes, that includes me."

"Why do you and they feel that way?" Martin asked.

"Well, for starters, he thinks he gets to dictate things that are really none of his damned business, such as forcing me to take down a welcome sign that hung outside our door for more than ten years ... until shortly after he became president. Then he put a note on our door saying we had forty-eight hours to take it down or he'd do so and dispose of it. Our granddaughter painted that sign, and it meant a lot to her and my wife to have it hanging there. After my wife died, it became even more important to me. I jotted a note on his note and taped it to his door. The next day I found that note back on my door. It said, 'Twenty-four hours and counting.' Nice, huh? The sign wasn't hurting anyone, and it was well done. It would be understandable if it was a piece of garbage."

"Why did he insist you take it down?" Martin asked.

"He decided we couldn't place or hang anything in the common areas. Now they look so sterile, so nondescript." Tim shook his head.

"Who else has complaints against Mr. Brooten?" Pete asked.

"Everyone who is having trouble affording the new monthly association fees. They have more than doubled since he got on the board. Some are afraid they will soon be beyond their means. The worst part is, with the current fees, it will be far more difficult to sell these condos. I told my son that when I'm gone, he should dump it for whatever he can get, because waiting for a reasonable offer will cost a fortune." Tim sighed.

"Why have the fees increased so much?" Pete asked.

"Because the board, and I believe that actually means Brooten, is doing all kinds of unnecessary things."

"Such as?" Pete asked.

"They trimmed all the trees to within an inch of their life. In the process, they destroyed the environment and eliminated the privacy the trees had provided for decades. Word has it, one of Brooten's friends was paid to do this. I was unable to get the name of the company. Doubt this friend has a company. Also doubt that friend was licensed, bonded, and insured. In other words, had there been a mishap, we could have lost our shirts in a claim against the association. I strongly suspect Brooten got a kickback on that job and several others." Scanlon's face went from olive to scarlet as he shared these details.

"Do any other members of this association hold that opinion?" Pete asked.

"I don't know. Haven't yet decided whether to pursue it."

"What kind of car are you driving these days?" Martin asked.

"Trying to determine if the getaway vehicle is mine?"

Pete snapped his fingers. "Tim Scanlon," he said. "You're a sergeant with the State Patrol."

"Was. I took early retirement to take care of my wife and be with her during her final days."

Pete saw Scanlon's eyes grow moist and said, "Sorry for your loss, Tim."

Scanlon closed his eyes and nodded.

After a respectful pause, Martin said, "Please humor us and tell us what kind of vehicle you drive."

"A 2016 red Highlander. Do I qualify?"

"Not even close," Martin said.

"Can you tell us which of your neighbors are Brooten's friends?"

"No. Sorry. I never see him hanging with anyone."

They thanked Tim and gave him their business cards, in case he thought of anything else.

As they were leaving, Pete glanced at his watch, then turned back and asked if they would be breaking a cardinal rule if they knocked on some doors, rather than going outside and ringing more doorbells.

Tim smiled and said, "The only one who would want to throw you over the railing for doing something so atrocious is no longer able to object. Go right ahead."

They only had about ten minutes until the VP said she'd be home, but they hadn't set specific times for their meetings with her or the treasurer, so the two investigators figured it wouldn't hurt to be a little late.

The first person to respond to their knocking was Kyle McGrath. He lived two floors below Scanlon. That was one floor below the one where Brooten had lived.

McGrath appeared to be in his mid-forties. He was a bit shy of six feet and, judging from his physique, he had a regular exercise regime. His wavy, light-brown hair was vacating his forehead. His blue eyes were piercing.

Before Pete or Martin could say anything, McGrath said he'd heard the police were talking to people about Fred Brooten, and he was tight on time. He had a zoom meeting scheduled to begin in twenty minutes.

That explains the dress shirt and tie with jeans and Asics running shoes, Pete thought.

After they introduced themselves, Kyle said, "I wanted Brooten out of here, however I wanted him to move, not die."

"Why is that?" Pete asked.

"I've never exchanged more than a few words with Brooten, but those conversations were always strained. The big point of contention was the amount of noise Brooten made as he wandered around his condo. Most infuriating was on Mondays through Fridays between 4:00 and 5:10 in the morning when, invariably, he woke me up.

"The guy sounded like an elephant as he walked around up there. I learned he had hardwood floors and offered to buy him area rugs, hoping that would at least muffle the sound. He said he had a roaming, self-propelled vacuum cleaner, so rugs would only screw things up for him. Then I offered to buy him padded slippers. Thought I might find some with thick soles, so I no longer heard every step he took. He said he only wore shoes. When I told him his walking around at 4:00 in the morning was disrupting my sleep, he crossed his arms, got in my face, looked down at me and told me to 'either live with it or invest in noise cancelling headphones.' I wanted to punch him in the gut, but he'd have either called the police or pounded me into the ground. After that, I avoided him. That wasn't difficult. Thankfully, I rarely saw him around here.

"Just so you know," Kyle added, "I moved in long before Brooten did, and neither the people who lived up there nor their family or friends walked heavily or stomped loud enough for me to hear them. So I don't think I was being unreasonable."

"Parking seems to be at a premium here," Pete said.

"That's because even two and three bedroom units come with only one garage."

"Since he woke you up every weekday, it would have been easy for you to follow him out of here anytime you decided you'd had enough," Pete said, carefully watching McGrath's face for a reaction.

Kyle's eyebrows moved closer to his receding hairline, and he looked Pete straight in the eye as he asked, "Are you asking if I followed him out of here this morning? First, I'd never resort to murder. Second, following him out of here strikes me as possibly the least efficient and effective way to get rid of him."

Pete and Martin asked for the names of neighbors who also had issues with Brooten.

McGrath said as best he knew everyone fit in that category. He claimed he didn't know enough to rank the severity of those issues. "Honestly," he said, "we don't like to talk about him. It gets us nowhere, and he makes our blood boil."

"What kind of car do you drive?" Pete asked.

"A Honda CR-V."

"Like it?" Pete asked.

"Yeah, but I'm regretting not getting a Toyota RAV4."

"Why?" Pete asked.

"They're both SUVs, but now that I own a CR-V, I like the appearance of the RAV4 better. I know, it's crazy."

When they told Kyle they were having trouble getting anyone to respond to their knocking, Kyle offered to call a friend who lived upstairs and next to the condo that had been Brooten's. He did, explained there were a couple of officers in his condo who really needed to speak with her, and she said to send them up.

They thanked McGrath and gave him business cards. "In case you hear anything that might help us," Pete said.

T hen they hiked back up two flights of stairs to Brooten's next-door neighbor, Debbie Ellsworth. Debbie looked to be somewhere in her seventies. She was of average height and build. Her gray hair was shoulder-length, her eyes were a blue green, and she wore a warm smile, gray sweats, and a headband.

Sally too had noise problems with Brooten, but this time he'd been the one who did the complaining, and he'd been obstinate about the noise he claimed she made. "He'd regularly pounded on his kitchen wall, which is on the other side of my living room wall," she said, "and he hollered that I had to turn down the volume on my TV. My hearing is good, and the volume is never higher than the medium setting. He had hearing aids, and must have had the volume maxed out. If I was bothering him, why didn't he just take them out or turn down the volume? He'd even pounded on the wall when I had family and friends over. None of them thought the volume was too loud."

"One day, I had to beg my son to ignore him. After Brooten pounded on the wall once too often, he wanted to go over there and punch him in the nose. My family keeps encouraging me to jump ship. The problem is, I have neither the energy nor the money to walk away from this place. I own it free and clear, but I could never get enough for it to buy something comparable and cover the costs of selling and moving."

Debbie sighed and shook her head. "Believe me, if I could ... Now that he's gone, I think my problem's been solved ... unless he has family members who are just like him and will move in now that he's gone. I think that would be criminal."

"I'll bet some of your family and friends would like to have made him evaporate," Martin said.

"Of course, but none of them would kill him. They all rely on prayer. Do you suppose their prayers were answered this morning?" she asked and winked.

Pete answered, "Possibly. But who did the dirty work?"

They gave her business cards and asked her to let them know if she heard anything that might help them.

"By the way," Pete said, "what kind of car do you drive, Debbie?"

"I no longer own a car, and I have a recommendation," she said. "Talk to Bernice Bethel. She knows everything about everything around here, including the comings and goings of all the residents, and who isn't getting along with who. She might be able to help." Before closing her door, Debbie smiled and waved good-bye.

On the way to their meeting with the board VP, Pete said, "Instead of hassling Debbie, why didn't Brooten get noise-cancelling headphones?"

"Because, based on what we've heard so far, he enjoyed flexing his muscles, intimidating people, and ordering them around. Do I sound unsympathetic to a victim?"

"Sounds more like you're listening to the people we speak with. However, since it hasn't been unanimous, we have to keep an open mind. Besides, it isn't our job to judge the victims, just find out who murdered them."

"Yeah, but do you find it surprising someone didn't pick him off sooner?" Martin asked.

"Well, thankfully, most of us don't solve our problems that way."

TWENTY-THREE
Cailyn Sobieski, Condo Association VP

Walking to the building where the Association's VP lived, Pete said, "I wonder if we'll need to make a trip to the management company to check on their payments and payees. If Lewiston is right, Brooten may have been playing the same sorts of games with the association's funds. More than one owner has voiced that suspicion."

"Well, at least that would make him consistent." Martin smiled.

"And if Hardwick ignores my instructions to email us the information I requested on the claims Brooten was involved in processing, he'll be a top priority tomorrow."

They called Cailyn Sobieski, the vice president of the board of directors, as they left Debbie's, and Cailyn was waiting for them at the door to her building. She was in her late sixties and just shy of five feet tall. What she lacked in height, she made up for in pounds. She had short, flame-red hair trimmed around her face. It accentuated her bright-blue eyes, and almost wrinkle-free face. She wore sweats, running shoes, and a smile.

As she opened the door, Cailyn said, "I heard about Fred. That's why you're here, right? You want to know if I know anything. A little while ago, my radio station started using his name. Until then, they kept calling him an unidentified man. I don't think Fred would have liked that."

Just when Pete and Martin began wondering if she'd stop long enough to take a breath and let one of them get a word in she said, "Sorry I'm such a jabber mouth. I'm just nervous about what is going to happen to this place without Fred. He was such a ball of energy, and he always had a project going. He accomplished so much that would never have happened without him."

Cailyn brushed away a tear. "The thing is, without him, I become the president. How am I going to replace Fred? I can't! I'm a nervous wreck. I'd never have let them name me the vice president had I thought this could happen."

She looks like she's on the verge of a nervous breakdown, Pete thought.

"There's no sense standing here," Cailyn added. "Let's go up to my condo and get comfortable. Would you like some coffee? Tea? Pop?"

Cailyn's condo was on the far right on the second floor. That gave her western and northern exposures. She had an elegant formal dining room set that was visible from the living room. The living room contained two beige recliners and a compact plaid sofa. There was room for little else, other than a couple of end tables. One stood alongside the sofa, the other between the recliners. She motioned Pete and Martin over to the recliners and asked again about beverages, saying, "I'm getting myself a Diet Coke and can just as easily get something for you."

Both men asked for a Diet Coke.

Seconds later, Cailyn delivered them, along with a couple of coasters. Then she sat down on the sofa and said, "What can you tell me about what happened to poor Fred?"

"At this time," Pete said, "now that the radio stations have announced his name, all we can tell you is what they've already told you."

She stared at Pete, then Martin, and looked like she wasn't buying that. After a long pause, she said, "But you have to know more than the radio stations. You're police officers. You have all the inside information."

"Currently, we're unable to disclose any additional details," Pete said. "I'm sure you wouldn't want us to compromise the investigation."

Hearing that, Cailyn's expression quickly transitioned from a tight-lipped frown to a smile, and she nodded in agreement.

"How long have you lived here, Cailyn?" Pete asked.

"Twelve years."

"Why did you seek a position on the board of directors?" Martin asked.

"Well, I didn't really, but a neighbor asked me, and I wanted to make a difference. It's so hard to get anyone to take an interest in anything around here, and it's almost impossible to get volunteers to fill the openings on the board. We're volunteers, you know." She sighed.

"Yes, we've heard. Why is it so difficult to get volunteers?" Martin asked.

"First, it's a thankless job. People either complain that nothing is getting done or they grumble about the cost of the things we accomplish."

"Who sets the priorities and the schedule for the things that are done?" Martin asked.

"The board."

"Do they have to get the approval of the owners?" Martin asked.

"Yes, when it comes to improvements, no when it comes to the maintenance and repairs."

"What differentiates improvements from maintenance and repairs?" Martin asked.

"Well, that seems to be a bit iffy. Typically, maintenance includes the things necessary to maintain the place, such as mowing the lawns and shoveling the driveways, parking lot, and sidewalk, and repairs covering essential things that are broken. Things that will cost us if not repaired. But for the last few years, we seem to have expanded those definitions to include things such as replacing functioning lighting fixtures and adding more, trimming tree branches that were not broken or hanging in the way of the lawn crew, things like that."

"So you're saying the difference between maintenance and repairs on one hand and improvements on the other is open to interpretation?" Martin asked.

"Well, Fred believed so."

"How about the owners?" Pete asked.

"Some of them disagreed, vehemently."

"Which owners?" Pete asked.

"Actually, I don't know. The complaints never came to me. I just know Fred used to get really angry about it."

"And he never said who'd made him angry?" Pete asked.

"I think he was angry with the owners as a group."

"The board had free reign when it came to the spending for maintenance and repairs?" Pete asked.

Cailyn stiffened up, scratched her head, thought a minute, then said, "We need it if we're going to keep this place running and in good shape."

"Are you quoting Fred?" Martin asked.

"Well ... not verbatim."

"Did anyone ever tell you they disagreed with any of the projects the board took on?" Martin asked.

"No. Maybe because many of the people around here are my friends."

"That makes sense," Pete said. "You're a good and kind person who wants to help make things better for them. Who selected the vendors?"

Cailyn relaxed a bit and said, "The management company usually gets bids, and sometimes someone, like Fred, makes recommendations. Often the contractors he recommends will do the service for a lower price."

"And you know that because?" Martin asked.

"Well," Cailyn stammered, "Fred told me."

"The people he finds who will do it for a lower price are always licensed, bonded, and insured?" Pete asked, going back to a concern mentioned by Tim Scanlon.

"They must be," Cailyn said. "Our governing documents require it, in order to protect us."

"Seems like an important provision," Pete said. Then he added, "Sounds like you and Fred used to talk a lot. Correct?"

Appearing on the verge of tears, Cailyn nodded.

"Did he ever mention being afraid of anyone?" Pete asked.

Cailyn shook her head and said, "I don't think he was afraid of anyone or anything, but now I am. If someone went after Fred, will they also come after me, since I am an officer of the association? If Fred's murder has to do with his being president, why stop with him?"

There was no way to answer, so standing, Pete said, "We greatly appreciate your time and cooperation, Cailyn ... and the Cokes."

He and Martin gave her their business cards and asked her to contact them if she thought of anything else, especially anyone who was angry with or had a grudge against Fred or the board.

TWENTY-FOUR
Sean Northrop, Condo Association Treasurer

Without verifying their identity, Sean buzzed in Pete and Martin when Martin rang the doorbell.

Martin said, "Heck, Northrop may have been expecting us, but he had no way of knowing we were the ones who rang the bell."

"You know, Martin, if I lived in a building with a security system, I'd want you to live in my building."

"Great! When should we start looking?"

"In about forty years, give or take."

"Heck, Pete, in another forty years, I'm planning for Michelle and me to move in with either Marty or Olivia." Martin laughed.

As they entered his building, the two investigators saw Sean on the stair landing above. He was in his late thirties or early forties and a handsome six footer with dishwater-blond hair and cobalt-blue eyes. He wore a charcoal-gray suit, white shirt, and navy tie. He smiled when he saw them and asked, "Peter Culnane?"

Without waiting for an answer, he continued, "I apologize for not returning your call. I've had nonstop meetings all day and thought I'd call when I got ready to head home. That's when you reached me."

Sean gestured for them to follow him up the stairs to his condo.

"What do you do for a living?" Pete asked.

"I'm a recruiter for 3M. It's a busy time of year for us, preparing for the next graduating class. We're anxious to recruit the best of the best. I guess that goes without saying, huh?"

"What background do you need for that job?" Pete asked.

"I have an MBA from Notre Dame."

"Impressive," Pete said.

"I imagine you've heard about Fred Brooten," Martin said, wanting to get things moving.

"Yes, thanks to at least a half-dozen voice messages on my cell."

"Reaction?" Martin asked.

"How about if we wait until we get settled inside my condo?"

"Fair enough, lead the way," Martin said.

Northrop lived on the third floor and in the apartment closest to the stairway. He opened the door and the two investigators entered the living room.

Sean's condo looked like the consummate bachelor pad, with a big-screen TV covering one wall, and two brown leather recliners facing it. Along the adjacent wall were a couple of upholstered, wingback chairs.

"Why did you choose to be the association's treasurer?" Martin asked.

"Actually, I didn't. It's more like they chose me. A friend who lives here put my name on the ballot unbeknownst to me, and I was elected. That election only put me on the board. None of the other members wanted to be the treasurer, in fact they refused to be, so here I am ... much to my chagrin."

"What does the job entail?" Pete asked.

"I keep track of the money in all association accounts and sign the checks. Sometimes, I have to recommend that the board increase the monthly dues for the members."

"I'll bet that earns you great adoration," Pete said.

"Death threats would be more accurate. Sorry, I shouldn't kid about that, in light of what's happened."

"Are increases in dues a regular occurrence?" Pete asked.

"I've lived here for eight years, but have only been on the board for three. My term expires in a little over a year, thankfully. There have been major increases in the fees for each of the last two years. Prior to that, the increases were, on average, every second year, and they were insignificant compared to the last two."

"How do you explain that?" Martin asked.

"A lot more projects than previously." Sean rolled his eyes.

"Projects?" Martin asked.

"New lighting, a lot more painting and tree trimming, things like that."

"In your opinion, do those projects justify the increases in fees?" Pete asked.

"Frankly, no. But I'm consistently overridden in my opposition. That's just one of the reasons I'll be glad when my term ends."

"What are the other reasons?" Pete asked.

"Winning through intimidation has been the modus operandi for the board for the last few years," Sean said.

"Perpetrated by anyone in particular?" Pete asked.

"Yes, the guy who died today. I feel bad he died, but quite honestly, I'm glad to have him out of my life. He snowed and intimidated members of the board so much that whatever he wanted was not only what happened but how it happened."

"Another member of the board told us he sometimes saved the association money by getting his friends to do some of the work around here," Martin said.

"He did, but I don't believe we saved a penny in the process. In fact, I think he created a lot of unnecessary jobs for those friends. In other words, we spent a lot of money we shouldn't have."

"Doesn't the membership vote on most improvements?" Martin asked.

"Only when the board of directors defines them as improvements. I challenged a few of those things, and was overruled. It's gotten to the point that I don't care what they do. I just don't want to be a part of it."

Sean shook his head and blew out a long breath.

"Was anyone else around here having problems with Fred Brooten?" Martin asked.

"Just about everyone who was paying attention."

"How about some names?" Martin asked.

"So I can sic you on them? Sorry, I won't do that."

"If you refuse to cooperate, we could haul you down to headquarters, you know," Martin said.

"Look I don't think anyone around here did it. There was no triggering event that I'm aware of. No big new projects, anything like that. And I'm not aware of anyone who is in financial straits yet, due to the increases in assessments. No one ever told me they wished he was dead. So I don't think I can help you in that department."

"We want a list of the 'friends' that Fred Brooten got work for around here," Pete said.

Sean frowned and said, "You don't need that right this minute, do you? I'd like to have a chance to unwind after a long day and eat dinner first."

"If we leave here without that information," Pete said, "do we have your assurance we'll have it by 8:00 tomorrow morning?"

Pete knew it was nearly 9:30. Not only should they let this guy get some dinner, but they'd put in almost a sixteen-hour day. Besides, other than knocking on more condo doors, and the answers were becoming repetitive, there was little they could do until tomorrow.

Sean nodded, then his face lit up and he said, "You think one of them might have killed him, huh?"

"We're checking out all possibilities," Pete said. "And the information you provide to us today needs to include the company name, the name of Fred's friend, the job or jobs they did, and the company address and phone number." He counted the items off on his fingers as he mentioned them.

"I don't think I have all that information for all of those people. Believe me, I tried, but the addresses were often post office boxes, and the company name was, as best I could tell, often just the friend's name. Also, there were times when Fred insisted I give him the check to deliver. I told him that was highly irregular, since he was an officer, but he didn't care. I don't even know if that's true. All I know is, it made me nervous."

"In that case," Pete said, "include the name of the bank or other institution where those checks were deposited or cashed and the organization whose stamp is on the back of the check. That might be the only way we can track some of those people."

"Just out of curiosity," Martin said, "does 3M provide you with a company car?"

"Yes, because I'm driving all over, recruiting."

"What kind of car?" Martin asked.

"A RAV4."

"Are you the reason Kyle McGrath decided he wanted one?" Martin asked.

"Yes, he's been lusting after my car ever since I got it." Sean laughed.

The two investigators stood, thanked Sean, and recited the rest of their departing ritual comments.

After Sean closed the door behind them, with his eyebrows raised, indicating a question, Martin tilted his head and flicked a thumb down the hall in the direction of the all-seeing, all-knowing Bernice Bethel's condo.

Bernice failed to answer their knock.

Taking it one step further, Pete called the phone number they were given. Standing outside her door, they heard the phone ring. Bernice didn't answer.

Both investigators wondered, *Where could she have gone that she'd leave her cell behind? Did she forget it?*

TWENTY-FIVE
9:30 PM, Homeward Bound

Exiting the building, Pete said, "I have some bad news, Martin."

Taken off guard, Martin stopped dead in his tracks and looked at him, concern painted across his face.

"I think we should hang it up for the day. If that doesn't sit well with you, go ahead and drop me off at my car, which I hope is still parked where we left it almost fifteen hours ago, and you can continue without me."

"Rather than risk showing you up, I'll call it a day." Martin laughed. Both investigators smiled when they saw Pete's unmarked car where he'd parked it.

Martin said, "I hope Teddy will be awake when you get home. Thanks for dinner, and I'll see you tomorrow. What do you think, 7:00?"

"No, 8:00 will be fine. The people we need to start with won't be available any earlier than that."

Before starting his car, Pete made two phone calls. The first was to "the all-seeing and all-knowing" Bernice Bethel at Brooten's condo complex. If she hadn't seen anything unusual this morning, he hoped there had been something in the recent past that raised her suspicions.

Unfortunately, if she had, he wouldn't hear about it tonight. His call went to voicemail. This time, he left a message. Then he called home.

When Katie answered, he said, "Control tower, this is Culnane. I'm making my final approach with an ETA of 10:00 CDT."

"That's wonderful, Culnane." Katie laughed. "Teddy is up, and I'm sure he will be when you arrive. I'll make sure he is."

Hearing the garage door open, Katie was at the back door when Pete walked in. She handed Teddy to him.

Pete had been mulling over the case on his way home and wore a frown, but that changed immediately when he saw the two of them. He held Teddy up over his head. Then he brought him face level and kissed his forehead. A second later, he gave Katie a quick peck on the lips. "More to follow," he said. He leaned down to pet Benji who was wiggling with excitement.

They played with Teddy, showing him high contrast flash cards and reading to him, then Pete rocked him to sleep, singing his favorite lullaby and cuddling with Teddy.

Meanwhile, Katie got ready for bed.

When Pete walked into their bedroom, she said, "You must be exhausted. You should get to bed."

"If I fall asleep right now, I'll get six-and-a-half hours of sleep. However, if I skip my morning run, I could get seven hours. But the run wakes me up and gets my blood flowing, so I'd be worse off. Are you planning to go to bed now?"

"That's what I was thinking, but ..."

"Give me five minutes to get ready, and I'll join you. I'd love to fall asleep with you in my arms."

"Me too." She smiled and kissed him.

Katie followed him into the bathroom. While he got ready for bed, she told him about her and Teddy's day. They both crawled into bed, happy that Pete made it home in time to make this possible.

During the night, they both got up each time Teddy woke up, and both did their part. After Katie nursed Teddy, Pete burped him, then rocked him the minute or so it took for him to fall back to sleep.

Pete woke up at 5:30, without an alarm clock, as always. He felt refreshed before and after his four-mile run. He showered, and Katie kept him company while he got ready for work. They ate breakfast together and spent some time with Teddy.

Katie, Teddy, and Benji accompanied Pete to the back door and sent him off with a hug, a kiss, and a wet hand.

TWENTY-SIX
Day Two

On the way to headquarters, Pete's mind raced back and forth between the new case and Katie and their baby. He was pleased how well, with Martin's help, he'd combined the two thus far. He couldn't anticipate things would go as well as yesterday, but even a few days like that would be a bonus.

Despite all the additions to his morning ritual, he parked his car and walked into his office at his usual time, seven o'clock.

The first thing he did was check his email. He was glad to find a message from the condo treasurer. He was not surprised to see there was no message from Joe Hardwick.

The email from Northrop contained an attachment, listing Brooten's "friends" who had done work for the condominium association. Pete was amazed by the number of "businesses" for which Sean had no address.

Sean's message said he'd highlighted in yellow the names he knew Brooten delivered at least one check to, and he'd highlighted in blue those which business names seemed highly suspect.

Next he went online to the Minnesota Secretary of State's website and checked to see if any of these "businesses" were registered with that office. Not one was listed. It was generally required for small businesses, and certainly added credibility.

Since a business should be aware of the benefits and the service was typically free, his doubts that these were valid businesses grew. The thing he couldn't understand was why the management company, namely George, didn't keep the association from contracting with these vendors. Had he tried, to no avail?

Having done as much in this department as he could for now, Pete switched gears to Brooten's professional career. Since Joe Hardwick hadn't sent an email, Pete knew the only way to force him to provide the information he'd requested was through a search warrant. He also knew they didn't have enough evidence to get one, so he thought about other options.

Wouldn't any officer of the corporation, with the exception of anyone involved in the scheme, want to know if one or more claims adjusters was fraudulently processing claims? How could they not?

In that case, the question was, how could he get to one of them and convince them to check out Lewiston's claims? He again found the list of officers for Fundamentals Insurance and examined the organizational chart. A vice president of the small business division seemed like a good starting point, unless that woman, Candice Hadley, was a coconspirator. How could he wrangle a meeting with her? Who knew her or another officer of the corporation who could arrange it for him? Who did he know who had some power in the business community?

Pete sat at his desk, rubbing his upper lip and running through all his connections. He started with family, went from there to friends, then people he'd met while working cases, and it finally came to him, *What about Palmer Comstock?*

Palmer Comstock was the retired CEO of Broughley, Inc., who was shot a few months ago on the way to his own retirement party. *Would he help? Would he mind being asked? Would he feel put out?*

Pete decided there was only one way to find out. He found the phone number in his files and decided he shouldn't call before 9:00 a.m.

As a backup, he also obtained the names and phone numbers of the members of Broughley's board of directors he and Martin had interviewed. He knew that some people belonged to the boards of several corporations. If he failed with Comstock, one of them might serve as a conduit.

Then Pete began planning his and Martin's day, starting with prioritizing the seven names on Northrop's list. It was 7:30, and he assumed most people with their own businesses were up by then, but decided to wait for Martin. In the meantime, he went through his notes from yesterday, making notations on them and adding notes to himself.

He was still doing this when Martin walked in at 7:45, smiling and carrying two Starbuck's coffees. "I got you a Grande dark roast, thinking you'd need a caffeine boost, and a Grande medium roast for me," he said, placing one in front of Pete. "But you look like you had a good night's sleep. Did you decide to check into a motel?"

"And risk Teddy calling in the middle of the night to ask where I was?" Pete laughed.

After telling Martin about his plan to call Palmer Comstock, he handed him a copy of Northrop's attachment and explained it.

"I'd like to just show up at those businesses," he said, "but if they are one- or two-person operations, we could waste a lot of time driving around for nothing. So let's call them and say we'd like to meet about a job. It'll be true, but highly misleading, since it'll be a job they already completed." Pete shrugged.

They called all the businesses on the list, and in several cases were given a different phone number. By 8:30, they'd reached all seven and had only three appointments for this morning. For the other four, they'd have to wait until the person got home from a job she or he was working. Since it was Friday, they were able to schedule those meetings, beginning in the early afternoon.

On the way to the first of these meetings, Pete called Palmer Comstock.

Palmer's wife, Pam, answered and seemed pleased to hear from Pete. "Palmer is doing great!" she said. "We haven't yet taken our trip. I'm still in remission, knock on wood, and we're waiting until all the hiking it requires won't be a problem for him. Would you like to talk to him? I'm sure he'd love to speak with you."

"Pete Culnane!" Palmer answered after picking up an extension. "Based on what I saw a few months ago, I trust you and your partner are keeping the streets safe for us. My family will never be able to thank you enough for determining who attacked me ... and making sure he could never do it again. What's up?"

"My partner and I could use your help, Palmer. A case we're working would benefit greatly if we got some assistance from an executive of a St. Paul company. We tried to get the needed information through the normal channels and ran into a brick wall. Do you know anyone in the upper echelons or on the board of Fundamentals Insurance? Anyone who might be able to pull a few strings for us when it comes to their small business division or gain access to that division's records?"

"Right off the top, no. But I'll bet I can find someone. Let me make a few calls and get back to you."

Pete thanked Palmer and said he'd be in and out of interviews, so if he didn't answer ...

"How did you ever think of calling him?" Martin asked as Pete disconnected.

"Dumb luck."

Martin rolled his eyes and said, "That'll be the day."

"I just tried to think of anyone I knew or had ever dealt with who might have connections with those in the top ranks of Minnesota companies. It took a while, but eventually I thought of him."

"Brilliant, and if his connections help us solve this case, it'll be like divine providence that we worked his case, then this one, and there turned out to be a critical link."

They were grabbing their overcoats when Pete's cell vibrated. It was Cailyn Sobieski. He put her on speaker, so Martin could hear. She was in a panic. "It looks like my concerns that other board members might be in danger was absolutely correct," she said, half out of breath. "There was a fire in my building first thing this morning. Lots of smoke. Everyone was evacuated safely, but that might not have happened. Thank goodness for the mandatory smoke alarms. I don't know what caused the fire. I do know I'm petrified. Called my daughter. She'll be picking me up shortly."

TWENTY-SEVEN
Richmond Tree Service

The first meeting on Friday morning was with Gene Richmond of Richmond Tree Service. His office was in his home, located on St. Paul's eastside. It was a compact ranch style with gray vinyl siding and white trim. Vegetation was scarce, with a bush growing below the picture window, and a lone oak in the back yard.

Pete paid close attention to the truck parked in the driveway and the cars parked along the street near the Richmond home.

Gene was in his fifties, with scraggly black hair, bushy eyebrows, and narrow brown eyes. He gave a new meaning to the term skinny. If he took his shirt off, Pete was sure he could count not only his ribs, but also the vertebrae in his spine. He wore ragged jeans, a long-sleeved T-shirt, and running shoes that had too many miles on them.

He looked questioningly at the two investigators as they introduced themselves, and his jaw dropped when Martin said they were there due to the death of Frederick Brooten.

"What happened to Fred?" Gene asked.

"He was attacked yesterday and died," Martin said.

Gene shook his head and said, "Oh, his poor family. What will they do without him?"

Either he knows nothing about Brooten's personal life, or he's intent on putting on a good show, Pete thought.

"No sense standing here. Let's talk in my office. Follow me," Gene said and led them through the living room to a bedroom that, based on square footage, barely qualified as one.

Filled wall-to-wall with a bedroom set, it didn't look like an office. However, jammed in one corner was a card table adorned with a computer, monitor, printer, and stacks of paper, plus a folding chair.

Looking around, Gene shrugged and said, "Guess we'll be too cramped in here. Let's meet in the living room."

If the Richmond Tree Service was a rousing success, the furnishings were no indication. The living room held little more than two black, IKEA-style, curved back chairs and a two-toned, gray-striped sofa.

Pete and Martin settled in the chairs, and Pete began the questioning, asking, "How long has Richmond Tree Service been a business?"

Gene rubbed the back of his neck, stared at the ceiling, rearranged himself on the sofa, then said, "Three years, give or take."

"When did you register with the Minnesota Secretary of State?"

"Huh?"

"You didn't do that?" Pete asked.

"Do I gotta?"

"You might want to check into it, Gene."

Martin took a turn, and started by asking, "What's your background and training?"

"Well ... got me a high school diploma, and I been working for more than twenty years."

"I mean, regarding your tree service."

"I couldn't have been more than ten when I started mowing the lawn and helping my dad trim the trees and shrubs."

"What did your dad do for a living?"

"He had a grocery store, back when a neighborhood grocery store could still survive. As a kid, I used to think I'd inherit it." Gene did a hands up shrug.

"Are you a certified arborist?" Martin asked.

"A what?"

"What classes have you taken in botany, plant physiology, soil science, pruning techniques, urban forestry, courses like that?" Martin asked, glad he'd done a google search after arranging this meeting.

"None, but those people charge a lot more than I do."

"So what qualifies you?" Martin asked.

"I've got all the necessary equipment."

"Such as?"

"A chain saw, an axe, and stuff like that."

"What kind of services does your company provide?" Pete asked.

"Mostly tree and bush trimming."

"Do you have a list of repeat customers?" Pete asked.

"No, but there's some places where I've been many times."

"How about a few of those names?" Pete asked.

"Well, there's the condos Fred managed."

"How many times have you done jobs there?" Martin asked.

"At least once a year for the last few years."

"Is your company licensed, bonded, and insured?" Pete asked.

"Huh? I don't know what you mean."

"How did you go about getting the jobs at that condo complex?" Martin asked.

"Fred got them for me."

"Did you have to bid on them?" Martin asked.

"No, like I said, Fred got them for me."

"How did you determine how much to charge?" Pete asked.

"I charged what Fred said to. He got me the jobs."

"Did you recommend what work needed doing?" Martin asked.

"No, Fred did."

"When it came to something like trimming the trees, did he tell you to trim them as needed, or did he tell you how high to go?" Pete asked, considering Tim Scanlon's comment about the tree trimming.

"Fred decided all those things. I disagreed one time. He got mad. Told me I owed him a lot and I should keep my mouth shut and do as he said."

"When did you do your last job there?" Pete asked.

"Last fall, and Fred told me I had to go back sometime this month."

"What do you need to do this month?" Pete asked.

"Don't know. I was waiting to hear."

"What do you do when your tree service doesn't keep you busy?" Pete asked.

"A little of this, a little of that. I can fix almost anything, and people who like what I do tell their friends. I get most of my business that way."

"Do you get most of your money that way or through your tree service?" Martin asked.

"Actually, that way."

"It must be profitable," Pete said, "I saw the BMW sitting out front."

"That's Lonny's baby. His wife almost threw him out when he brought it home."

"What do you drive?" Pete asked.

"I need a truck for my business. The Tacoma sitting in my driveway, of course."

"You're a one-car family?" Pete asked.

"Yup, I'm a one person one-car family. If I come home with a BMW, ain't no one going to throw me out." Gene grinned, by all indications happy with that arrangement.

"What made you decide to start a tree service?" Martin asked.

"Fred told me to."

"How much did he charge you for the jobs he got for you?" Pete asked.

"What are you talking about? I'm the one who did all the work," Gene shouted, thrusting his thumb at his chest.

"True, but without Fred's help, you wouldn't have gotten a lot of the work and made the money, right?" Pete said.

Gene silently chewed on his lower lip, clenching and unclenching his fists.

"You can tell us, Gene," Pete said. "We understand it's sometimes the price of doing business."

"Twenty-five percent. He always got twenty-five percent. After a while, he wanted more, but I told him no way in hell. He said he could bring an end to my work for his association, and I told him I wouldn't pay him more, no matter what."

"Like you told us," Martin said, "you did all the work. Did it make you mad when he wanted more money?"

"Naw. That was Fred."

"How long have you known him?" Martin asked.

Gene scratched his chin and thought for a while, then said, "At least ten years, but I don't even know. I fixed a lawnmower for him."

"Did Fred have any enemies?" Pete asked.

"How would I know? We never talked much, and I doubt he'd have told me anyway. I know he'd never admit being afraid of anyone. He wanted everyone to think he was fearless."

As soon as they were out the door, Pete pulled out his cell and checked the number that had caused it to vibrate during that meeting. Before breaking into a run, he held the phone out, so Martin could read the caller ID.

TWENTY-EIGHT
Johnson and Company, Interior Decorators

Martin was right on his heels and hit the unlock button before Pete reached the unmarked car.

Pete didn't spend the time required to retrieve and listen to the voicemail message. Instead, he touched the phone number he recognized at the top of his phone's listing of recent calls.

Palmer Comstock answered saying, "So, Pete, you got my message."

"Actually, no. I saw the phone number and called."

"Not a wasted minute, huh? You remind me of myself in my working days. I got a contact for you. Her name is Alex Villard," Palmer said and recited the phone number. "She's a VP, but not in the division you mentioned, and she's the friend of a friend. I spoke with her. Told her I'd appreciate her listening to what you had to say and helping if she could. I also told her I respect your opinions and your instincts. She's expecting to hear from you. If you strike out with Alex, please get back to me. I'll find someone else. Glad you called. This is the most fun I've had in weeks. Good luck, Pete."

Pete didn't wait. With fingers crossed, he dialed Alex's number.

She said she'd expected to hear from him and offered to meet with him and Martin at her office on the seventh floor of the Wells Fargo Building at 11:00 that morning.

That left time for the meeting scheduled with Ray Johnson, the owner of Johnson and Company Interior Decorators.

They drove to Johnson's home in St. Paul's Como Park area, which Johnson explained was the base of his operations. On the way, Pete texted Kurt Worthington, asking him to call ASAP. He hoped there was a way to get information on the claim Kurt said Brooten monkeyed with before their meeting with Alex Villard.

Ray Johnson's home was a beige stucco ranch-style with multi-colored beige brick from ground to roof to the left of the front door. The house was tucked in a neighborhood of many of the same, as well as two-story traditionals. All were circa 1960s.

Johnson was in his late sixties, of average height, and solidly built. He had thick white hair and brown eyes. His face was so pale, it resembled chalk. He wore white pants flecked with a variety of colors of paint, a turtleneck shirt, and a grayish-blue sweatshirt. Like his pants, his shoes were flecked with paint. Judging from the size of his shoulders, hauling paint around and the types of motions required to paint for many hours a day were great ways to build muscle.

After they introduced themselves, Ray got them situated in his living room. Based on the house and the furnishings, his business was far more successful than the Richmond Tree Service, or he didn't mind living beyond his means. The floors were honey-oak hardwood. On the far wall was a fireplace of tan brick that ran from floor to ceiling. Left of and in front of a five-panel picture window was a navy velour sofa. Kitty-corner to the sofa were two medium-blue, twill oversized chairs.

Martin took the lead, asking, "Have you been watching the news? Have you heard about Frederick Brooten?"

"Yeah, just heard about him on the radio. If you're here about him, I assume you haven't caught whoever did it."

"No, sir, we haven't," Martin said. "You and he were friends?" Martin asked.

"More like business acquaintances."

"How did you meet?" Pete asked.

"I painted the home of a friend of his. The guy liked my work and recommended me. For more than two years, Fred has had me on hold to paint his place. He keeps putting me off."

"What was his friend's name?" Pete asked.

"Max Austin."

"Where does Max live?" Pete asked.

"He and his wife have a nice home in Shoreview."

"Do you know what he and/or his wife do for a living?" Pete asked.

"I may have heard, but I didn't pay much attention."

"You must have Austin's phone number," Pete said.

"Yes, but not at my fingertips."

Ray must have been organized, because at Pete's request, he left the room, and it took only a few minutes for him to find it. When he returned, Ray handed Pete a slip of paper listing Austin's name, address, and phone number.

"When's the last time you heard from Fred?" Pete asked.

"Last fall."

"Was that regarding the painting of his place?" Pete asked.

"No."

"Then what?" Martin asked.

"For the last few years, I've been painting the common areas in the condominium complex where he lives. He often stopped by to see how it was going."

"Someone told us Fred said he was advised to have the common areas painted every two years. Are you the person who advised that?" Pete asked.

Ray lurched forward in his chair and asked, "Are you calling me a crook?"

"Are you saying that recommending that would be dishonest or self-serving?" Pete asked.

"I'm saying it's total nonsense, and that's exactly what I told Fred. He said there was nothing he could do about it, because that was what the board of directors wanted. I knew it was a waste of money and even offered to speak to the board of directors. He said it would be a waste of their time and mine. He also told me to keep my mouth shut if any of the owners told me they thought it was a waste, because that would be the last time the board contracted with me."

"Did any of the residents ever say anything?" Pete asked.

"Once in a while, someone would ask if I thought painting every other year was overdoing it, and I'd just shrug."

"Were you required to submit a bid every year?" Martin asked.

"No, I never submitted one. Fred said he'd take care of it to make sure they didn't settle for inferior quality. He said as the president of the board, he had the authority. I'd never heard of anything like it, but it was guaranteed, steady work, and I was able to set my own schedule."

"Who set the price?" Martin asked.

"I did."

"Is your company licensed, bonded, and insured?" Martin asked.

Fred looked at Martin like he was some kind of idiot and said, "Of course!"

"In return for the assured work, did Fred expect you to paint his place for nothing?" Martin asked.

"If he did, he never said so. And unless it was a small room and he'd removed all the furniture and done all the preliminaries, I'd have refused."

"What if he'd threatened to get a different painter for the common areas if you didn't do it?" Pete asked.

"I don't like being threatened. I'd have told him to take a flying leap."

"But what about the loss of work?" Pete asked.

"There's plenty of work out there."

"I suppose you need a pickup truck or something comparable to haul around ladders, paint, tarps, etcetera," Martin said.

Ray nodded.

"So you need a second vehicle for other times, huh?" Martin asked.

"No. My pickup suffices, and it cleans up nicely ... whenever necessary." Ray shrugged.

"Did you ever see him with friends or did he ever mention friends, other than the one in Shoreview?" Pete asked.

"Nope."

"How about enemies? Any idea who might have been after him?"

"Not a clue." Ray shrugged and added, "But I didn't really know him."

The two investigators gave Ray their business cards, just in case, and hurried off to their meeting with Alex.

Twenty-Nine
Fundamentals VP Alex Villard

Ever the optimist, Pete checked his cell as soon as he reached the car, even though it hadn't vibrated during the meeting with Johnson. He was disappointed, but not surprised, to see there was neither a text nor a missed call from Kurt Worthington, the guy Brooten had still been supervising and who believed he was on the take.

Then he said, "Do you believe Johnson, Martin?"

"Not a chance. Why would Brooten require all the common areas to be painted every two years if there was nothing in it for him?"

"Exactly. But for now, we have no way of proving it."

When they reached downtown St. Paul, Martin parked again at a fifteen-minute meter on Seventh Street, and he and Pete caught an elevator to the seventh floor in the Wells Fargo Building.

This time, the receptionist was a friendly woman in her twenties who smiled the moment they arrived. The smile stayed put while she got the name of the person they wanted to see and called her.

In little more than a minute, Alex came out and greeted them. She was an attractive woman in her late fifties and of medium height and build. She wore her gray hair in a short hairdo that accentuated her small features, and her hazel eyes shone through glasses with heavy brown frames. She wore a medium-gray, wool-crepe pantsuit and a robin's-egg blue, crew neck sweater, a pearl necklace and earrings.

Smiling, she introduced herself and shook Pete and Martin's hands, then she led them back to her office. The plaque on the wall outside the door said, Alexandra Villard, Vice President, Health Insurance Division.

Her office was large enough to swallow Pete's in one gulp, and the windows provided a gorgeous view of the State Capitol complex. Her mahogany desk had only a few, neatly arranged stacks of paper. Her computer wasn't visible, but the monitor was large enough to watch movies on ... without missing anything. Photos and plants decorated the windowsill. Four chairs were arranged in a circle in one corner of the room, and two padded, leather chairs faced her desk.

"Can I get you anything to drink?" she asked.

Both men declined, not wanting anything to delay the start of this meeting.

After getting situated in the grouping of four chairs, Alex said, "A friend called this morning and asked for a favor. She wanted me to meet with you and help you if I could. What is it you'd like me to do?"

Pete said, "Are you aware that a man who had been a claims adjuster for Fundamentals Insurance was murdered yesterday?"

"Yes, Frederick Brooten. A company-wide email was sent yesterday."

"Do you mind if I ask who sent it?" Pete asked.

"No, it was his supervisor, Joseph Hardwick."

"My partner and I are investigating that murder, and it has come to our attention that there's a possibility Frederick Brooten fraudulently processed some claims. If that's true, and I'm not saying it is, there's a chance those actions contributed to or resulted in his death, and that's the reason we requested this meeting."

"Fundamentals Insurance Incorporated prides itself in the services we provide, including the accuracy of our claims processing. We take any allegations of fraud very seriously. What led you to believe one of our employees is guilty of fraud?"

"We suspect fraud may have occurred," Pete said. "We aren't alleging it did. We wanted to meet with you to request that you run some checks to prove or disprove our suspicions. The basis for our suspicions is, a former employee of Fundamentals Insurance discovered changes were made to a claim he negotiated and finalized. He worked for Frederick Brooten and asked to meet with him to discuss those changes. Brooten refused and fired him. He believes the changes made were inaccurate and in fact highly suspect."

"It could be sour grapes, you know. It wouldn't be the first time someone reacted that way to a dismissal."

"We agree," Martin said. "But rather than letting it go at that, we have the names of a couple of claimants and would like someone to go over those claims, looking for irregularities."

"And if there are?" Alex asked.

"We want to know about it. Regardless, for the purposes of this investigation, we'd like the contact information for all the claims Brooten and his staff were currently working on, settled or were involved in the settlement of for the last three years. You see, if he was fraudulently negotiating settlements for personal gain, he may have gotten himself into a predicament from which there was no escape."

"I know you won't be surprised to hear that we aren't happy to have someone suggest one of our adjusters would or could do that." Alex frowned.

"We do understand," Pete said. "But we think it behooves your company to investigate the allegations in order to determine whether they are true and, if they are, decide how best to proceed."

"It seems the logical place to start is with Frederick Brooten's supervisor," Alex said. "I can ask him to review the claims you believe may be questionable." How does that sound?"

"I realize that sounds like a good starting point," Pete said. "But what if his supervisor was somehow also involved?"

"Are you suggesting the problem may go all the way to the top?"

"No," Pete said, "but we'd rather not take a chance. Could you, for example, find someone in another division who was a claims adjuster, is still familiar with the processes, but is now working in another area of the company?"

"That's an interesting plan of attack." Alex smiled for the first time since this discussion began. "But it would have to be someone we could trust not to share what we are doing or the findings." She closed her eyes and rubbed her cheek. "That could take a few hours."

"If there's a problem, finding it now and addressing it will no doubt be painful for Fundamentals Insurance," Pete said. "But it will be far better business-wise, including when it comes to the public image and reputation you've worked hard to create and maintain."

"Of course, and if you're right, I'm taken aback that we were so vulnerable in this area." Walking over to her desk and waking up her computer, Alex asked, "What specifics can you give me about the claims you believe may have been handled fraudulently?"

Pete recited the names of the two companies whose claims Wayne Lewiston contested, as well as the types of things he questioned and the differences in the totals for the settlements.

Alex entered that information into her computer as fast as he uttered it.

When she'd finished, Pete said, "A third claim was brought to our attention by a different adjuster. Unfortunately, we don't yet have the details for that one. Is it okay if I get back to you when I do?"

Alex sighed and said, "Please do."

"I imagine," he added, "that inevitably there will be differences in the calculations of the totals done by different people, since adjusters are making judgments throughout the process, right?"

"Absolutely, and we'll keep that in mind. I'll find someone to go through the claims with a fine-tooth comb today. Plan on hearing from me."

THIRTY
Austin Roofing

"I'm glad we met with her, rather than the VP for small business," Pete said as they left the seventh floor.

"And how. What if the problems go all the way to the top, and the VP of the small business division had her fingers in the pie?"

"Well, depending on the type of pie, that might provide the perfect clue. For example, if it was a blueberry pie, her fingers might be purple."

Martin just shook his head. Then while Pete tried again to reach the "all-seeing" Bernice Bethel, Martin called Austin, another person on the condo treasurer's list.

Pete struck out.

Martin hit a homerun. Disconnecting, he told Pete, "Austin's office is in downtown Lake Elmo. He said he'd be there and available until 1:30. Do you suppose he'll buy us lunch?"

"That might depend on how happy or unhappy he is about Brooten's death."

"In other words, will he be a member of the group that thought Brooten was the best thing since sliced white bread, or the group that thought he was lower than dirt."

"Precisely."

During the twenty minutes it took to get to Lake Elmo, they discussed how to attack the information Alex would provide about all the contracts Brooten had his fingers in over the last three years.

"I'm thinking we should create a spreadsheet," Pete said. "The fields would cover the company name, address, contact person, et cetera. As the information comes in, another would show the amount of the discrepancy, if there was one. That way, we could rearrange the companies, based on that rank order. The thing we have to be careful of is thinking the largest discrepancies are the best bet. Assuming there was fraud, we have no way of knowing that Brooten treated these claimants equally."

"Looking at all the people we've spoken with," Martin said, "that might be especially true for the condo contractors. Take Richmond Tree Service. For someone like Gene Richmond, it was huge."

When they reached Lake Elmo's main street, which ran about a quarter mile, they found a variety of businesses, most in standalone buildings. Austin Roofing was located in an impressive old bank building, dating back to about the time of John Dillinger and updated in the 1960s.

As they pulled up in front, Pete said, "Do you realize that until this case we never found ourselves having to enter a building that was once a bank? Now, this is our second in two days. If I was superstitious, I might think there was some significance."

"Will you become superstitious if the banks play a key role in solving this one?"

Smiling, Pete said, "Ask me after we solve it."

Entering the building, they saw a receptionist to their left. *She looks just like my third grade teacher,* Martin thought.

Walking up, they told her they wanted to speak with Max Austin.

"Is one of you Martin Tierney?" she asked.

Martin felt like raising his hand, but nodded instead.

Motioning in the direction of several barrel-shaped upholstered chairs to her right, she told them to have a seat while she got Max.

A short time later, a man in his late forties who was well over six feet tall, had a barrel chest, jet-black hair and mustache, and deep-set brown eyes walked up to them. He wore dress slacks, a white dress shirt, and a striped tie. His rolled up shirtsleeves displayed muscular forearms. Extending a hand in their direction, he asked, "Martin Tierney?"

Martin rose, shook his hand, and said, "You must be Max Austin."

When Max nodded, he introduced Pete, and Max led them back to his office.

An executive-style oak desk with two 24-inch monitors was the centerpiece. Four large, comfortable upholstered chairs arranged around a circular conference table completed the room.

Whereas some executives would have planted themselves behind the desk to show who was in control, Max walked over to the conference table. "It's going on noon, and I usually order in my lunch," he said. "Can I get the two of you anything? I recommend both the corned beef sandwich and the cobb salad with roquefort dressing."

"That would be nice," Pete said and hoped eating together would put Max at ease.

Both Pete and Martin thought the salad sounded better, but ordered the corned beef sandwich, since it would be easier to eat while conducting the interview.

Austin walked to his desk, punched in a number, and placed the order. Returning to Pete and Martin, he said, "Okay, what's this all about?"

"I don't know if you read a newspaper or how much attention you pay to the news, but Frederick Brooten was murdered yesterday," Pete said, while he and Martin carefully studied Austin's face for a reaction.

"Yeah, I saw it on the news last night," he said, and his facial expression revealed nothing, not a sense of loss nor one of relief, nor an attempt to mask another reaction.

"We understand you were friends," Pete said.

Austin smiled and said, "That's laughable. The only person I can imagine telling you that is Brooten himself, but I have a feeling you haven't spoken with him. Have you?"

Martin answered his question with a question. "How would you characterize your relationship?" he asked.

"He attempted to establish a business relationship with me, and I turned him down."

"Please explain," Martin said.

"He had a house in West St. Paul he wanted to sell, but first had to fix the roof. I don't know how he got my name, but he asked me for an estimate. When I gave it to him, he told me he could make it worthwhile for me if I did it gratis.

"I asked how he thought he could accomplish that, and he took me to this condominium complex where he lived. He said he could get me the contract to reroof all eight buildings, if I did as he asked. I asked when the shingles were last replaced, and he had no idea. So I took my ladder off my truck and checked two of the roofs. When I finished, I told him there was no way those buildings would need to be reroofed for at least another ten years, barring something like hail damage.

"So he told me he was an insurance adjuster, and he had all kinds of opportunities to steer the businesses for claims he approved in my direction. That, of course, seemed legit and a good source of business. I didn't repair his roof for free, but I didn't blow him off. He took a handful of my business cards, and said I'd be hearing from him.

"Several months later, a hailstorm went through the southern suburbs. I heard from a business owner whose roof was damaged and was looking for a contractor. He told me that Fred Brooten referred him.

"I made an appointment to check out the job and give him an estimate. Before I got out the door, Brooten called and asked if I'd heard from that guy. I said yes, and he was all jolly, reminding me he'd said he could be good for my business. Then came the real reason for his call. He said he could approve the roof for a higher reimbursement if I only agree to work with him. I asked what that meant, and he said I could bid the job at say 120 percent, and all I had to do was give him half of the overage. I hung up and called the guy who had requested the bid, said something had come up, and I wouldn't have the staff for his job for at least a year. I refused to take a chance on getting the bid and having Brooten on my back, insisting I owed him. A few times after that, someone called and said they were referred by Brooten. I was always too busy."

"How long ago did all of that happen?" Martin asked.

"Roughly two years ago."

"Did you ever think about reporting him to his company or ..." Pete asked.

"Thought about it, but never did. I don't have the time or energy to take on someone like him."

"When was the last time you heard from one of Brooten's referrals?" Martin asked.

As Austin opened his mouth to answer, a woman brought in the lunch order. He stood, reached in a pocket, and pulled out a money clip. Pete stood simultaneously, saying, "We appreciate you placing the order for us, but I insist on buying mine and Martin's."

Austin shrugged, took the check, did the calculations, and Pete paid him.

After the delivery person left, without needing Martin to repeat the question, Austin smiled and said, "I'm happy to say, it's been more than a year since I was last contacted by one of his referrals, and let's eat. We can talk around our food."

Rather than doing that, they spoke between mouthfuls.

"Have you heard from Brooten since then?" Pete asked.

"He left a couple of voice messages on my cell, saying he had a new deal for me. I never returned those calls."

"My guess is," Pete said, "Brooten would have driven you stark raving mad, had you taken him up on his offer."

Austin finished chewing and said, "That's why I'm so grateful to have had honest, church-going parents who would spin in their graves if I ever did something so unethical."

"Amen to that," Martin said.

"I understand you live in Shoreview," Pete said. "This is a long way to drive each day for work."

"True, but at least I'm traveling in the opposite direction from the majority of the traffic."

"A fuel-efficient vehicle is probably important to you," Pete said.

"It is. That's why I leave the truck here and drive my Nissan Leaf to and from home."

"Since it probably sits in the sun most of the time, did you get a light-colored one, so you wouldn't bake while it cooled down?" Pete asked.

"Well, almost. It's silver."

"My wife and I have looked off and on for a new home," Pete said. "I imagine in your line of work you see a lot of what's out there. Can you recommend a suburb or a neighborhood?" Pete asked.

"Where do you live now?"

"Maplewood."

"Shoreview is nice, but I don't think we have anything over Maplewood, if you're thinking the same general price range."

"Ah yes, the old price-range problem." Pete smiled.

"By any chance, have you heard of any other businesspeople who have dealt with Brooten?"

"No, but if anyone had asked me, I'd have told them to run as fast as they could in the opposite direction."

Pete and Martin thanked Max and, just in case, gave him their business cards.

"Whoever did it probably did the world a favor," Austin said. "But I know we can't let that influence you, so good luck."

THIRTY-ONE
Covering All the Angles

"**F**rederick Brooten was a real piece of work, wasn't he?" Martin said, walking down the sidewalk from Austin's office to the unmarked car.

"It seems he was bent on playing all the angles," Pete said. "I wonder how many of the people he worked a deal with ended up blackmailing him, or vice versa. And we may have found an explanation for all the cash Forensics found in his condo. I don't imagine he'd have wanted Austin writing a check for his cut."

"But how would Austin have handled it tax-wise? At least if he wrote Brooten a check, he could write it off as a business expense—I think. This isn't exactly my area of expertise."

"Nor mine. That's why God created accountants."

"Good to know." Martin laughed. "No word from Kurt Worthington? I thought maybe he'd use his lunch break to contact you."

"Nothing yet, but he could still be on his lunch break."

On the trip back to St. Paul, Pete tried again to reach Bernice Bethel ... and failed.

"You know, Martin, something doesn't feel right about this. I can't explain it, but I have this uncomfortable feeling about her."

"What can we do, other than call one or both of the people who mentioned her and ask if they know if something's up with her?"

"That might be a good idea. We don't know how old she is, and what if she needs help and can't get to a phone?"

Pete's vibrating phone interrupted the discussion. It was Worthington, and he gave Pete the name of the company whose claim he'd processed and Brooten modified, as well as the types of modifications he made."

After thanking him, Pete called Alex. It was 12:45, and he wondered if she'd be at lunch.

Alex was there and happy to hear from him. She was still searching for someone to examine the claims Pete and Martin had already provided, but was happy to have the final one—or what was the final one for now.

"It's a Friday afternoon," she said, "but I'm still confident we can complete the evaluation of those three cases today. I hope to get back to you by mid-to late-afternoon."

THIRTY-TWO
Amina Ali's Cleaning Service

After sharing Alex's comments with Martin, Pete said, "We won't contact any of the businesses Wayne and Kurt told us about, until Alex tells us whether or not there were problems with the settlements.

"Let's get back to the list Northrop provided, showing Brooten's coconspirators who contracted with the condominium association."

The next person they interviewed was Amina Ali. Her company took care of the floors at Brooten's condo complex.

Amina lived in a neighborhood of one- and two-story houses, circa the 1960s, located in North St. Paul.

Her home was a basic two-story with pale-yellow vinyl siding above waist-high beige brick, dark-brown trim, doors and shutters, and an attached two-car garage.

She was a slender five foot one with black hair, dark-brown eyes, and coffee-colored skin. Ali wore a green running suit and black quilted slippers. Opening the door, she stepped back so they could enter. Through a thick Somali accent, she asked why they wanted to talk.

"Do you know a man named Frederick Brooten?" Pete asked.

Ali pulled her arms in tight across her chest and, in a small voice said, "Yes. Why?"

"He died yesterday morning," Martin said.

Ali's eyes went wide, and her hand shot up, covering her mouth.

"You haven't heard anything about it, like on the news or from family?" Martin asked.

She shook her head rapidly, side to side.

"We are here because you knew him," Martin said. "We understand he helped you get a job cleaning the floors at the condominiums where he lived."

Ali nodded repeatedly.

"Did he expect more from you than just doing that job, because he helped you get it?" Pete asked.

Again, Ali's nods were a replica of the motion of a bobble head doll.

"He wanted me to clean his apartment two times every month."

"Did you do that?" Martin asked.

Ali shook her head and said, "He would not give me a key. He wanted me to clean when he was home. I did not want to be alone with him. I was afraid."

"But you are still cleaning the floors at that complex, right?" Martin asked.

She nodded repeatedly.

"What did Fred Brooten say when you refused to clean his apartment?" Martin asked.

"He said I would change my mind," Ali said nervously.

"What did he mean?" Pete asked.

"I do not know. I was afraid to find out."

"How long ago did he tell you that?" Pete asked.

"Last year. Before Labor Day."

"Do you have a contract to take care of the floors for that association?" Martin asked.

Ali nodded.

"Can you tell us when that contract ends, when you will have to sign another?" Martin asked.

"Yes, in September."

"Was it the first time you signed a contract with them?" Pete asked.

"Yes. Because of what he said, I did not think there would be a contract. One day I was vacuuming, and he said to sign it. He was unhappy it took so long to read it. Before that, because of what he told me, I thought I would do the work every week, and they would pay me."

"How did you know him?" Martin asked.

"I do not know him!" she protested. "I was cleaning skyway windows downtown. He came to me and said he had an easier job that paid lots more. He told me what to charge and the number to call. He was right. The pay is lots more than they pay to clean skyways. Now I do both." She smiled.

"Why do you think he helped you?" Martin asked.

"I do not know. I asked my cousin. She said to smile and be glad. When he told me I must also clean his apartment, I knew. I did not trust him. I would not do it even if I lose that job."

It seemed nonsensical, but Martin asked what kind of car she drove.

"A red Toyota Corolla."

THIRTY-THREE
From Floors to Grass and Snow

The two investigators went from floors in North St. Paul to grass in the Hamline-Midway neighborhood, to snow in Highland Park. In the process, they went from a Somali woman to a Hispanic man, to a white man, indicative of the diversity in the Twin Cities.

Carlos Sanchez, a Hispanic man who lived near Hamline University, had a lawn service. His home was a well-kept, traditional two-story built in the 1930s. The landscaping showed his professional expertise and pride in it. His oversized, two-car detached garage was visible from the street.

It was obvious he'd been watching for them when he exited the garage and made his way to them as they approached the front steps.

Carlos was five feet seven with an average build, shiny black hair, brown eyes, olive-colored skin, and a broad smile. He wore a padded jean jacket over blue jeans and a sweatshirt. After reaching out a hand to Martin, he quickly withdrew it and apologized. "Sorry about the grease. Been busy, getting all the equipment set. Can't depend on the chill to last. Have to be ready when the grass takes off. Mind if we talk out here? I'd have to shower and change clothes to sit anywhere inside the house."

"As long as you're comfortable talking out here, we're fine with it," Martin said.

"No problem. Other than me, no one is home yet."

He'd heard about Brooten. "Makes me nervous," he said. "You no longer know which streets are safe and when. This seems like a safe neighborhood, but things can change so fast."

Fred had approached him while he was mowing the lawn at another condominium complex and said his condominium's management company told him about Carlos's company.

Fred suggested he bid on the upcoming contract, asking him to take a look at the complex and let him know how much he'd charge. As was the case with Max Austin, Fred pressured Sanchez to increase his bid by 20 percent, then split the extra amount he'd make with him.

Like Johnson, Sanchez balked. He submitted his original estimate and got the contract anyway. Carlos said after that, any time Fred saw him, he shook his head and said some version of, "At this rate, you'll always be a loser."

Carlos smiled and said, "I'd rather be a loser than have to be looking for the tax man or woman every time I turned around."

"Did he ever approach you with another offer?" Martin asked.

"No, I think he knew I didn't play those games."

"Did he ever threaten you?" Martin asked.

"How could he? If I'd done what he told me to do, he might have found a lot of ways."

"But he could have done something like claim your equipment damaged some of the bushes, curbs, buildings, or something else," Pete said.

"It would have been a lie, and he could never prove it."

Aside from a lot of riding lawnmowers, Sanchez's only vehicle was a Ford truck, and his wife drove an almond-colored Volkswagen Passat.

Burke Chandler, the snow removal contractor, was next on their list. He lived in a typical Highland Park home. It was a beautifully maintained, white with navy-blue trim, two-story traditional built in the 1940s, and included a front porch and a detached garage.

With wavy, light-brown hair, blue eyes, and a cleft chin, Chandler appeared to be in his late forties or early fifties. He was five feet ten and built like he'd shoveled a lot of snow. Black jeans and a navy, wool sweater completed the picture of a man who still drew a lot of attention from women.

"Mind if we meet on the porch?" he asked. "My wife has bridge club. Otherwise I'll have to parade you past them to the family room in the basement. I mean that literally. They'll all be checking you out."

Both investigators were happy with that arrangement, and none of the men bothered to sit on the furniture that still wore it's protective sheeting.

Subsequent to a Brooten sales pitch, Chandler had contracted with the condominium association for snow removal, and proudly described his business to the two investigators.

"There are two types of contracts," he explained. "The most common is a fixed rate for the season. The second is based on the number of inches of snow plowed.

"I'm always amazed by the people who try to save money by selecting the second," he said. "A few people did that this year and regretted it. In St. Paul, our average seasonal snowfall is around forty inches. This year, we got a little over ninety-seven inches. That's almost twenty inches more than last year, which was also well above average. During years like those, all that snow eats away at the margins, so I appreciate people who reject the fixed rate." Burke smiled.

"To stay occupied, in the off season I repair and replace driveways. I prefer pavers, but also do blacktop. The first is much more expensive, and the second is much dirtier work."

Burke said he read about Brooten in the morning paper. "Obviously, whoever did it knew his schedule and route. Family?" he asked. "Based on my dealings with him, they probably had plenty of reasons to get rid of him."

"Tell us about your dealings with him," Pete said.

"He was as crooked as a dog's hind leg."

"How so?" Pete asked.

"The guy was forever playing both sides against the middle."

"Specifically?" Pete asked.

After jamming his hands in his pockets, Chandler told yet another version of Austin's and Sanchez's story. And again, Brooten claimed if he cooperated, he had connections and would send a lot of business his way. "He was willing to screw his neighbors, monetarily, to line his pockets. I came right out and told him I run a legal and honest business, and would continue to do that. Do you think someone he coerced killed him? If someone took the bait, likely as not Brooten would have found a way to make them regret it."

"Do you know anyone else who did business with him?" Martin asked.

"First, I *never* did business with him. My contract is with his association, not him. And I'm happy to say I don't know anyone else who has dealt with him. Rest assured, if anyone mentioned his name, I'd have done my best to steer them away from him."

Chandler drove a pickup truck, and his wife drove a Honda Pilot SUV.

Like Austin, he thought Brooten's death was no loss to mankind.

When Chandler was out of earshot, Martin said, "By all indications, Brooten was an equal-opportunity thief."

Reaching the car, Pete felt his cell vibrate, indicating an incoming call. It was 4:46.

THIRTY-FOUR
Answers from Alex

Pete's incoming call was from Alex, and he smiled when he answered, hoping this meant she had answers for them, regarding the claims Brooten may have processed fraudulently.

Without bothering with a greeting, Alex said, "I have some bad news ... for me, but it may, in fact, be good news for you. All three claims you brought to my attention were fraudulent, and in exactly the ways you mentioned.

"Shortly, I'll be meeting with our president. I'm trying to determine the best way to drop this bomb. Wish me luck. I'll need it. I want you to know how much I appreciate you bringing this to my attention. Also, we will continue auditing all the claims that Brooten had a hand in, and I'll let you know about any others with discrepancies. Thanks again, Pete, and please thank Martin for me."

"You may want to think about doing something for the main person responsible for this discovery. He's a young man who is just getting started," Pete said. "His name is Wayne Lewiston, and he's been stuck doing minimum wage jobs ever since Brooten fired him, exacerbated by the negative recommendations Brooten provided when he applied anywhere. I realize it could be problematic to hire him back, but perhaps you know someone at another insurance company who could use a conscientious and ethical person like him in their ranks. If so, you may want to see what you can do. I hope you'll consider it."

"You're right, and I'm glad you mentioned it. My head is swimming right now, and it didn't occur to me."

As soon as he'd shared Alex's findings with Martin, they called the two companies Wayne mentioned and the one provided by Kurt, intent on meeting with as many of them as possible that day. It was a Friday afternoon in April, albeit an abnormally cold April day, and they failed to reach a single contact at their places of business. Rather than giving up, they called all of the other phone numbers they had for these companies, and the result was the same.

Regardless of the season, rush hour began around 1:00 on Fridays in the Twin Cities, as hordes of people headed north to lake country.

Is that why we had to meet with the last three people at their homes? Is that why we can't reach anyone on our new list? Pete wondered.

Trying to find a way around that potential problem, Martin searched for the home addresses for the contact people from Horizon Laundry, BPC Pet Hospital, and Wayne Lewiston's discovery, Everett's' Bar and Grill. While he did that, Pete searched for a salve for the nervous feeling he had about Bernice Bethel.

First he called Bernice's phone, hoping for a quick fix. No such luck. Again his call was sent to her voicemail. Unwilling to let it go at that, he decided to call one or both of the people who recommended Bernice as a good resource for him and Martin.

He started with Debbie Ellsworth. When she answered, he asked if she'd spoken with Bernice in the last day or so.

"No, and I'm concerned. I've neither seen nor heard from her since Fred was murdered. Kathy Wheaton saw her briefly late yesterday morning, but no one has seen her since then. She's always out and about, talking to everyone. Even more alarming is the fact she isn't answering her cellphone or returning any calls. Bernice hasn't done that for as long as I've known her. I'm so worried."

"Might she have taken off for a few days to visit family or friends?"

"Not without telling me."

"Any chance you have contact information for her family and friends who don't live in your complex?"

"Yes, she gave me all that, just in case ..."

"Would you do me a favor, Debbie? Would you contact those people, in case she left in a hurry and didn't have a chance to tell you?"

"That's a good idea. Just sitting on my hands is making me a nervous wreck. I'm so glad you called. I'll make those calls and get back to you as soon as I've finished, Detective Culnane."

THIRTY-FIVE
Next Steps

Continuing to wait to hear from Debbie about her friend, "the all-seeing" Bernice, he assisted Martin with his research. Internet searches helped them locate the correct person with two of the three companies named by Kurt and Wayne. These people were now their top priority. Perhaps since the amounts were significantly larger than those from Brooten's dealings with the people connected to his condo, he was even more manipulative, demanding, coercive, etcetera.

"What are your thoughts, Pete? It's a little after 5:00. Shall we drop in on the one closest to here and see if they invite us for dinner ... or at least Diet Cokes?"

"Let's give Debbie a bit more time to locate Bernice. I hope she isn't carrying on a long conversation with everyone on her list. If she is, I may not hear from her for another hour or two." Pete shook his head.

"Either way, are you planning to drop in on at least one of these businesses tonight?" Martin asked, wondering if the old Pete Culnane was sitting across the desk from him. If so, they would.

"Well ..." was all Pete got out before his phone vibrated. He smiled with relief when he saw it was

Debbie and answered, saying, "How did you make out, Debbie?"

"No one has heard from her since 11:00 yesterday morning. Not her family and not a single friend. Several called and said she didn't return their calls. I called Kathy, and she said Bernice was walking out of the complex when she saw her late yesterday morning. Since Bernice often goes on walks, she didn't think anything of it. I have a key. Do you think we should go check on her? She gave it to me for safety reasons, and I'm sure she won't be mad if it turns out to be nothing."

"That's a great idea, Debbie. Why don't you get back to me after you do?"

"I'm afraid to go alone. Will you and your partner come with me? I could ask another owner, but I'd feel safer if it was someone young and strong, like the two of you."

Pete thought about telling her there wouldn't be anyone in Bernice's apartment who could hurt her. But as farfetched as it seemed, he couldn't guarantee it. "We will be there in fifteen minutes," he said. "We'll meet you at your entry. Be sure to wear a jacket."

I sound like I'm talking to a five-year-old, he thought, *but she sounds so rattled, I don't know that she's doing anything other than reacting right now.*

"Thank you so much! I'll see you in fifteen minutes. Drive carefully, please."

Pete and Martin grabbed their overcoats and ran to Martin's unmarked car.

Thirty-Six
What about Bernice Bethel?

Pete and Martin parked close to Debbie's entrance. She stood just inside the door, looking frightened, nervous, desperate. "I just know it's something bad," she said. "I can feel it. It's like there's darkness all around me. Please, let's go check."

Bernice lived in the building to the right of Debbie's. Debbie had a key for not only Bernice's apartment, but also for the entrance into that building. Pete and Martin had to practically jog to keep up with her as she led the way to Bernice's building. Shakily, she slid the key in the lock then ran up the two flights to Bernice's floor.

Pausing outside Bernice's condo, eyebrows raised, she put her ear close to the door and listened, trying to detect any sound. Then she knocked on the door and did it again.

Turning to Pete, she said, "I don't have my phone. Can you call her?"

When Pete did, all three of them heard it ringing.

Debbie gasped and covered her mouth. "You don't suppose she died and is lying there, do you?" she whispered, looking like she was on the verge of tears.

"Let's stay positive, okay?" Pete said.

Debbie smiled weakly and nodded.

When the phone stopped ringing, Debbie inserted Bernice's key into the lock, turned it, and slowly opened the door.

There were no sounds—not those of a windup clock or a forgotten radio or television. And the only light came from the sunlight filtering into Bernice's condo, but it was enough to see the whole living room.

No sign of Bernice.

"Bernice?" Debbie called, probably louder than was necessary had Bernice been there.

"Shall we walk around and check the other rooms?" Pete asked.

"Yes, please," Debbie whispered.

With Debbie clutching Pete's arm, the three of them walked to the kitchen, where they had to turn on the light to see anything. Then they went down the hall to Debbie's bedroom, guest room, and bathroom. Her bed was made, and nothing looked out of place or disturbed.

"Let's go back to the kitchen and look around," Debbie said, continuing to whisper.

On Bernice's table, she found a small piece of paper. And on that paper was a series of letters and numbers, with three, a break, then three more.

"Looks like a license plate number," Martin said.

Debbie picked up Bernice's phone and, to Pete and Martin's surprise, entered her password.

Seeing their expressions, she said, "Bernice gave me her password, so I could call her family and friends if anything happened to her. She has mine for that same reason."

Turning her attention back to the phone, she checked Bernice's recent calls. There were three types: those that showed the caller's name, and that was most of them, Pete's calls that displayed as Blocked, and one phone number. That number appeared three times. She shared that with Pete and Martin.

"Are the calls showing that number incoming or outgoing?" Pete asked.

After completing several additional steps, Debbie looked up and said, "All outgoing. I wonder who she was calling, and why she didn't add them to her contacts. Should I call the number?"

"Let's hold off on that for a bit," Pete said.

"Any idea what she might have been doing with this license plate number?" Pete asked.

Debbie shook her head.

"Did she frequently leave her phone at home when she went out?" Martin asked.

"No, never! She always wanted it with her, in case of an emergency, like if she fell."

"Can you think of a reason she might have left it here this time?" Martin asked.

Debbie shook her head, and her eyes grew moist.

"Martin, would you please call Regions and make sure she isn't there?" Pete asked. "Just in case also ask about any unidentified patients who arrived in the last thirty-six hours. If you strike out there, broaden the search to other hospitals, including United."

"Will do."

While Martin did that, Pete checked to see if there was a license plate issued in Minnesota with the letter-number combination shown on Bernice's note. There was, and he got the name and address.

"Do you know if Bernice knows someone named Daniel Kimball?"

Debbie shook her head.

"Did she ever mention a Daniel or a Dan or anyone named Kimball?"

"No, and I'm good with names."

"Can you think of any reason she might have written down his license plate number?"

"I can't imagine, unless the car almost hit her when she was out walking. She put on a lot of miles."

"But what good would it have done her to have the license plate number, Debbie?"

"I shouldn't tell you this, but she has a longtime friend who works at Driver Vehicle Services. That friend might look it up for her. She may want to write a stinging letter to the driver. But you can't tell *anyone*! Bernice will be so mad at me if I get her friend in trouble."

"Do you know that friend's name?"

"I don't think I should tell you."

"Okay, since you know her name, you can find her phone number in Bernice's contacts, right?"

"I imagine so."

"Okay, first, check to see if she's one of the people Bernice contacted recently."

Debbie did, and found Bernice called that friend at 7:30 yesterday morning.

"Okay, hang on," Pete said and called Kathy Wheaton. He asked her if she spoke with Bernice early yesterday, such as before 8:00.

Kathy said she called Bernice at about 7:00. "She's always up at the crack of dawn," Kathy said, "and I wanted to brighten her day. I told her the police were here, asking about Brooten's family, and the only time you do that is when someone is murdered, right?"

When Pete didn't respond, Kathy continued, "Bernice hates Brooten, so I thought it would cheer her up."

"Why does she need cheering up?" Pete asked.

"Well, it isn't really my place to say."

"We're trying to find her, and it may help."

"Okay, fine," she answered reluctantly. "She's having some financial problems, thanks to the rapid increases in the cost of things, such as our monthly association dues."

Pete thanked her and disconnected, wondering if Bernice had been in a position to attempt something and was foolish enough to do it. He hoped not.

Then he told Debbie, "We need some information, and Bernice's friend who works at DVS might be very helpful. Would you call her and tell her you have a very important question and promise not to get her in trouble if she tells you the truth? If she agrees, give her the license plate number on that slip of paper, and say you're just making sure Bernice got that owner's name and address correctly."

"But what if she won't help?"

"Tell her in that case that her supervisor might find out what she did."

"If I was her, that would definitely scare the answers out of me," Debbie said.

While Debbie did as Pete requested, he thought about calling Alex and asking her to go back to work. If she did, he wanted her to check whether a Daniel Kimball was the owner or contact person for a claim settled by Fundamentals Insurance and in which Brooten was involved. But he decided that would be jumping the gun, and asking her to go in on a Saturday was probably no worse than asking her to do that on a Friday night, after a particularly stressful day.

Bernice's DVS friend told Debbie that Bernice called her yesterday, before she left for work, and begged her to get the information on the license plate number shown on that piece of paper. Bernice told her it was important to know right away whose car that was, since the owner always parked in her alternate spot, and it was a huge problem for her friends, many of whom no longer came to visit, because of him.

Bernice's friend looked up the number as soon as she got to work, then took a bathroom break and called Bernice with the information.

Hanging up, Debbie said, "That's strange. We don't have an alternate parking spot. It would be nice, but the builder figured there were enough spaces in the lot, so we didn't need one. He was wrong! What do you think Bernice was up to?"

Pete had a few ideas, but hoped he was wrong. So he just shrugged and said, "Let's check Bernice's text messages."

Debbie found one to the phone number Bernice called three times yesterday. It said, "Don't get cute. Won't have my keys. Your name and license plate number are on my dining room table. My phone is there too."

"Do you see her keys anywhere?" Pete asked.

Debbie scanned the counters, looked on top of the refrigerator and microwave, but didn't find them. Then she snapped her fingers, opened the drawer next to the kitchen sink, pulled out a keychain with four keys, and said, "The big, thick one is for the security door at the entrance, the two regular-sized ones are for her door and deadbolt, and the little one is for her mailbox. Why would she leave without them? I have her only other set."

"She must have known she could count on you to let her in, don't you agree?"

Debbie shrugged and said, "It still makes no sense to me."

"Well, when she gets back, you can ask her. Do you have a photo of her?"

Debbie gasped and said so quickly her words were almost unintelligible, "Do you think you need one to identify her remains?"

"Are you always this pessimistic?"

Debbie pulled tissues out of her pocket, blotted her eyes, and blew her nose.

"You can't think that way. Think of all the tears you'll waste. Do you have one?"

Debbie closed her eyes and bit her lip in concentration, then shook her head.

"Not even a selfie?"

"Oh, yes, of course, but I don't know how to send it to you. My son always has to do that for me."

Pete had her locate the photo, and hand him her phone. Then he texted the photo to himself and deleted the text, removing his phone number from her phone.

"You've been a great help, Debbie," Pete said. "We'll walk you back to your building. Why don't you make yourself a hot mug of tea and try to relax? Martin and I will check out the address she got from her DVS friend."

"Can't I go with you? What if Bernice needs me?"

"Are you suggesting Martin and I can't handle this?"

Debbie blushed and said, "I'd never think that. You'll call and let me know as soon as you find her, won't you?"

"This could take quite some time. There are a lot of steps involved. We'll let you know as soon as we can. Do you have a landline?"

Debbie nodded.

"Great, that will be the best way to notify you." ... *and keep you home, instead of driving to the address you may remember, since you're so good with names,* Pete thought.

Debbie gave him the number for her landline, and he wrote it in his notepad.

He and Martin walked her back to her building, thanked her, and both gave her a hug, hoping it would help calm her nerves.

On the way out the door, Pete said, "Bernice is lucky to have you as a friend, Debbie." ... *or was lucky,* he thought, hoping that wasn't the case.

THIRTY-SEVEN
Find Bernice

Tempting as it was, Pete and Martin didn't run to the unmarked car. For all they knew, Debbie was watching them, and they didn't want to risk sending her into cardiac arrest. It was also tempting to jump in the car and drive right to the address they had for Kimball. But they weren't a couple of cowboys. Both investigators knew they had to think things through and plan their strategy.

While walking from Bernice's condo to Debbie's, Pete had a change of heart. He called Alex Villard as soon as he reached the unmarked car. He wanted to know if Daniel Kimball had ever filed a claim with her company. If so, had Brooten been involved in it? If the answers to both questions was yes, knowing the key details might also be helpful.

He was surprised how quickly she answered.

"Alex," he said, "I hesitate to ask this of you tonight, but I'm hoping you'll do me a big favor. Would you go back downtown and search to see if someone named Daniel Kimball was involved in a claim filed with your company?"

"I'm still downtown, working to identify any claims Brooten had a hand in. Hang on, Pete. This will only take a minute."

After a brief pause, she said, "Yes, I have it on my screen. Kimball is the owner of a company called Kimball Computers. It says here they repair computers and sell refurbished ones. They're located in a stand-alone building in Highland Park. Three years ago, a fire destroyed much of the exterior and all of the contents. It took six months to negotiate the settlement. Frederick Brooten was the claims adjuster. Someone with the expertise will have to determine if there was fraud in that case."

"Is six months longer than the norm?" he asked.

"Sorry, I don't know."

Pete told her he'd appreciate it if they moved the Kimball case up in the queue and let him know when they'd examined it. Then he said he was happy to have reached her and appreciated all she was doing.

While Pete was on the phone with Alex, Martin arranged to have triangulation performed to determine the whereabouts of Daniel Kimball's cellphone. They did this by establishing the locations of the cell towers receiving his phone's signal, and comparing the strength of those signals. The more towers receiving his signal, the more explicit the location. So if he was still in the metro area, they'd be far better off than if he'd taken off for the hinterlands. For triangulation to work, of course, his phone had to be turned on. Martin crossed his fingers. The process was quick, once initiated, and he anxiously awaited the results.

He'd little more than completed that request when Pete ended his call to Alex.

They were comparing notes when Martin got the triangulation report. It showed Kimball's phone was at the address Pete had for him.

Sharing in Debbie's concern, Martin started the car, and they sped to that address in the Hiawatha neighborhood of Minneapolis, not far from Minnehaha Falls.

Martin followed Dale Street south to I-94, then went west, taking the Cretin-Vandalia exit and going south on Cretin to Ford Parkway. Traveling west on Ford Parkway, he crossed the bridge and soon arrived in Kimball's neighborhood.

During the trip, Pete checked to see if Bernice Bethel had a driver's license or Minnesota ID. She had a license, and he downloaded the photo and shared it with Martin.

Both men were concerned. On the way they discussed how they'd proceed after reaching their destination.

"I'm just thinking out loud," Martin said. "Right now, we have no real basis for believing Kimball is involved in Brooten's murder. Yes, he filed a claim with Fundamentals Insurance, and yes Brooten was involved in the processing. But Alex doesn't yet know if that one was fraudulent.

"The Bernice Bethel part is at least curious and, worst case, ominous," he continued, "but we also have no way of knowing the connection she has to him."

"Exactly," Pete said. "She could have his license plate number for a reason that has nothing to do with Brooten or this case. But my gut tells me something serious is going on, and it is related to this case."

As they crossed the Ford Parkway Bridge, Pete checked to see if the triangulation still showed Kimball was at home.

Both men nodded when the answer was yes.

"This is his street," Martin said. "Based on his address, he lives on the left side."

"How about driving past so we can determine which house and scout out the neighborhood?" Pete suggested. "Then you can go around the block, drop me off, continue past his house, and take up a position where you can see if he leaves the house and heads for the garage or runs. You probably won't be able to see the complete left and right sides of the house, as well as the back, but if he comes running towards the front of the house, I'll see him."

"I like it." Martin smiled.

Daniel Kimball's home was in the middle of the block. He lived in a tidy, brick two-story with a covered entryway that was four steps up from the street. A detached, one-car garage was accessed from the alley. Carefully trimmed shrubs stood below the picture windows, and a large oak shaded the front of the home during the summer.

As they passed, both investigators wondered why all of the visible window coverings were closed. Was Kimball trying to hide something?

After completing their inspection pass, Martin dropped off Pete at the corner. That gave Martin enough time to park and walk to either Kimball's garage or a neighbor's, depending on which provided the best vantage point.

Getting out of the car, Pete unbuttoned his overcoat and laid it on the backseat.

"It's that warm?" Martin asked.

The temperature's a little above forty, but there's no wind." Patting his shoulder holster through his suitcoat he added, "I want to be prepared, eliminate any impediments to quick access."

"Text me when you're ready. I won't ring the doorbell until you do and, when he opens the door, I'll speak loud enough for you to hear and join me."

"What if a plane is taking off or landing at that precise moment?"

"Excellent question, partner. If one is, I'll wait until the noise diminishes so Kimball and you can hear me."

He gave Martin a thumbs up, closed the car door, and made his way to Kimball's. He walked like he was on a Sunday stroll, except he carefully examined everything along the way. When he reached Kimball's home, he didn't regret seeing the drapes were still closed ... and there was no sign someone was peeking around them. Had someone been doing that, they had to be either psychic or paranoid.

After quietly ascending the four steps, he positioned himself to the right of the door with his back to the brick wall ... just in case, and waited for his cell to vibrate.

Following Pete's lead, Martin left his overcoat in the back seat. The neighborhood seemed dead for a Friday night, but maybe everyone was out to dinner, partying, or just vegging at the end of a long week. He walked slower than he would have liked to avoid alarming anyone or raising their suspicions. When he reached Kimball's garage, he checked out the view from a few angles. Not happy with any of them, he walked the scant distance to a neighbor's garage. Standing behind it and looking around the corner as inconspicuously as possible, he decided he now had a better view of the back and sides of Kimball's home, as well as of his garage. Sweating, and glad his overcoat was in the car, he texted Pete.

Pete got Martin's text during an all-too-brief lull in the air traffic. Staying put alongside the door, he reached down and rang the doorbell.

THIRTY-EIGHT

Introductions to Bernice and Friend

When the ringing doorbell elicited no detectable response, Pete prayed the break in takeoffs and landings would last at least another minute or two. With his ear turned toward the door, he thought he heard whispering, and considered shouting, "Police, open up."

Would that elicit the worst possible kind of response? He rang the doorbell a second time, then waited and listened.

This time he was sure he heard some shuffling around and wondered if Kimball was about to run. Waiting for a second, possibly frantic text from Martin ... or a phone call, he stayed put.

Suddenly, a deep voice said, "If there's someone out there, where are you hiding? I can't see you through the peephole."

"Doing his best imitation of a prepubescent boy, Pete said. "Give me a break. I can't help it I'm so short."

He was surprised when the next thing he heard was the metallic sound of the deadbolt sliding open. Hand inside his suitcoat and on his Glock, he remained alongside the door ... a less-accessible target.

Next he heard the door scraping on the rubber cushion that kept out the hot and cold air. When he heard the same masculine voice say, "What the hell?," Pete stepped out and said, "Police, Mr. Kimball," in a voice so loud, Kimball had to wonder what was wrong with his hearing.

He'd only completed about half of that when a plane circled overhead, preparing to land at the Minneapolis-St. Paul International Airport. Holding up a finger, he pointed skyward, indicating he'd wait until the noise diminished ... and Martin joined him, he hoped.

When both happened, he said, "My partner and I got your name from Fundamentals Insurance Incorporated. We need to talk to you about one of their employees, Frederick Brooten. Would you describe your interactions with him?"

"Why do you care? I heard on the news that he died."

"That doesn't change anything. It's still important to know as much as possible about his dealings."

"Got an ID?"

Pete and Martin pulled and held out their badges and IDs.

"Fine, come in. But why all the shenanigans? Why did you have to hide and make me think it was a neighbor kid playing a prank? I mean, it is Friday night."

"Sorry, Mr. Kimball," Pete said. "We were afraid that after a long week you might not be interested in talking to anyone other than family and friends."

"I have company, but come on in," he frowned, waving them inside.

They knew from his driver's license that Daniel Kimball was forty-one, six feet tall, and 175 pounds, but he looked ten years older and twenty pounds lighter. He had wavy brown hair and haggard-looking blue eyes. He wore khakis, a Minnesota Timberwolves sweatshirt, and moccasins.

The first thing the two investigators saw was an older woman, sitting in an aged recliner with her legs up and wearing a smile. Yes, it was Bernice. Per her license, she was seventy-nine, five feet eight, and 120 pounds. She had short, wavy, salt-and-pepper hair, and sharp hazel eyes. She wore khakis, a turtleneck, and a royal blue crew-necked sweater.

All of the living room furniture, including the recliner, appeared to be about two decades old, but cared for and clean. The television sitting on a simple metal stand appeared to be of the same vintage, which made it ancient by current standards.

"Mind introducing us to your friend?" Pete asked.

While Daniel did so, Bernice lowered her legs, stood, and walked briskly over to the three men. She continued to smile as she shook hands.

She's agile, moves lake an athlete and has a warm, firm grip, Pete thought. *If she's a hostage, either Kimball has brainwashed her or she's suffering from Stockholm Syndrome. If it's the latter, this must set the record for the least time required.*

"Mrs. Bethel," he said.

She stopped him and said, "Call me Bernice."

Pete smiled and said, "Bernice, we've spoken with several of your friends. One of them, Debbie, is very concerned, because she hasn't seen you, and you haven't answered your phone or responded to her messages."

"Debbie is a natural born worrier."

"Do you know her number?" Martin asked. "If you do, you should at least call and tell her there's no need to worry."

"Danny, can I use your phone?"

"On the wall in the kitchen, Bernie, but you already know that. Go ahead and call her."

While Bernice called Debbie, Pete and Martin told Kimball they wanted him to come to headquarters with them. "We'll be able to interview you more readily there than here," Pete said, "due to your proximity to the airport."

He and Martin were surprised when Kimball sighed, nodded, and said, "If necessary. But I do have a question. Are you accusing me of something?"

THIRTY-NINE
Taking a Ride Downtown

When Pete told him they had no basis for accusing him of anything, Kimball relaxed for the first time, including easing the tight line of his mouth.

Suddenly Martin remembered the unmarked car was parked half a block away and around a corner. To avoid the questions that was sure to raise, he told Kimball it often took a while to start the car, so he'd get it going before they were ready to leave. It wasn't the best story he'd ever concocted, but Daniel nodded, seeming to buy it.

Exiting through the front door, Martin ran all the way to the car, hoping he'd be in front of Daniel's home in time.

Martin's departure seemed to light a fire under Daniel, who stood and walked over to the living room closet. As he opened the door, Pete saw the contents were limited to a winter jacket, a raincoat, a windbreaker, a woman's winter coat, a pair of shoes, a pair of boots, plus a shelf holding a variety of gloves, baseball caps, and stocking caps.

That supports the other indications he lives alone, Pete thought.

Daniel sat on the floor, slid off his moccasins, and put on the shoes. Then he stood and pulled the winter jacket off the hanger carefully enough to avoid dislodging the hanger.

As he did so, Bernice returned to the living room.

"I'm going to headquarters with them," Daniel said.

"Why?" she asked.

"It's no big deal. They just have some questions."

"Why not ask you the questions right here?"

"We talked about it. It's fine, Bernie. Let it go, okay?"

"Okay, but I don't like it."

Observing this, Pete thought, *She could be more of a problem than he.*

Returning to the closet for Bernice's coat, Daniel said, "They can take you home on the way. Sorry we didn't have time for dinner. I'll make it up to you the next time." Then whispering in her ear he added, "So glad you called and came over, and we had a chance to talk. You worked wonders on my emotional state."

Pete couldn't hear that exchange but, based on Daniel's attitude, their facial expressions, and the brevity, he wasn't concerned that they were conniving.

Daniel held Bernice's coat for her, and as soon as she had it on she gave him a big, protracted hug and kissed his cheek.

For the first time since he'd arrived, Pete saw Daniel smile. He didn't correct Daniel's erroneous statement that they'd take Bernice home before they went to headquarters. They'd deal with that and her reaction closer to HQ.

For the first time today, Pete wished he and Martin weren't traveling in the same car. It would be easier if they separated Daniel and Bernice, and each took one. Fortunately, it wasn't an insurmountable problem.

Standing alongside the unmarked car, breathing still a bit labored and waiting for everyone, Martin faced west, toward the house, and saw the setting sun. The sky was filled with streaks of red, pink, and orange, interspersed with shades of blue and a few white wisps of cloud. Gazing appreciatively out of the corner of his eye, he saw Pete, Daniel, and Bernice walk out the front door and down the steps toward him. Martin's focus shifted instantaneously.

Pete opened the front passenger door and said, "Bernice."

While she got settled, he opened the rear passenger door and said, "Here you go, Mr. Kimball."

"What about you?" Daniel asked.

"I'll come around to the other door and be sitting back there with you." Pete smiled.

"Why don't Danny and I ride together in the back?" Bernice asked.

"Why don't you relax and enjoy the ride?" Pete said.

"Is that what you tell everyone on the ten most wanted list?" Bernice asked, oozing sarcasm.

After insuring they were buckled in, Pete walked around the car and got in behind Martin.

Martin put the car in gear and began the trip to HQ, hoping Daniel didn't have a change of heart on the way. Both he and Pete thought Bernice would go along with their plan to question her at headquarters, if Kimball didn't object.

They'd know in about twenty minutes.

FORTY
Flip a Coin

While Pete and Martin remained on high alert, it was an uneventful trip from the Hiawatha neighborhood of Minneapolis to headquarters, until they approached the Dale Street exit off eastbound I-94. It was the first and probably most logical exit to take to get to Bernice's condo.

When Martin failed to move into the exit lane, she said, "Have I become invisible? This next exit is mine."

Martin slammed a fist on the steering wheel and conjured up his best imitation of utter obliviousness as he said, "Sorry, Bernice. I was under the impression that you knew we need your help as well as Daniel's. We're trying to develop a complete and accurate picture of Frederick Brooten. Daniel dealt with him as the representative of an insurance company and is helping us with those aspects. Your experiences with him are as a member of your condominium association, and several of your neighbors recommended we speak with you. We tried repeatedly, but failed to reach you. Will you come to headquarters now and help us?"

Guess he took acting lessons while I was on paternity leave, Pete thought, hoping Bernice bought the performance.

"Which neighbors?" Bernice demanded.

"Debbie, for starters, but what difference does that make?" Martin asked.

"I'm getting hungry," she said grouchily.

"We'd be happy to treat you to any taste sensations the best vending machines offer. Will that suffice for now?" Martin asked.

Bernice threw up her hands and said, "Fine. I'd hate to be the bane of your existence."

"Wonderful. Thanks," Martin said.

Ten minutes later, the four of them stood in front of a line of vending machines, making some difficult decisions.

Bernice settled for a bottle of water, granola, and Biscotti cookies. "All the basic food groups." She smiled.

Daniel chose a Coke, mixed nuts, and pretzels.

Both investigators got a Diet Coke, hoping for something more substantial either at home or at a restaurant, after they finished with these interviews.

Although there were benefits to interviewing each of them first, they decided to start with Bernice. Kimball had been less reluctant to come to headquarters, and, based on their interactions thus far, he was far more patient. If necessary, they could split them up and each interview one, but they were reluctant to do that, because the likelihood was great that what they learned while interviewing one would be beneficial while interviewing the other.

Neither was surprised when Bernice fought that decision. She said she didn't have to get right home, and insisted they interview Danny first. "Got a newspaper?" she asked. "I haven't read today's edition, and I haven't seen the crossword. Between the two, I'll be busy until it's my turn."

Adjusting for that change in plans, they split up the work. Pete set up Interview Room 1 and got Daniel settled there. Martin took Bernice to Interview Room 2, found her a copy of today's *Star Tribune*, then joined Pete and Daniel.

They hadn't discussed Brooten's murder with or in front of Bernice, but Martin figured she had to know about it, since Kimball did. He wondered, *was that the real reason she wanted to see the newspaper? Did she want to know what it said about Brooten and the murder?*

FORTY-ONE
Daniel Kimball

Kimball didn't appear anxious or nervous, but Pete started the interview with something innocuous, in case it was an act. "Tell us about your business, Daniel," he said.

"Well, I repair and sell computers, including many I've refurbished. I also sell accessories, because I can buy them in quantities and still make a profit while beating the online prices."

"I can barely turn on my computer," Martin said. "How do you know so much about them?"

"My degree is in computer hardware and software, and I'd originally planned to be a programmer. In no time flat, I knew forty hours per week of that was not for me. I got a lot of satisfaction out of fixing the problems I often had with my own computer. When you spend untold hours trying everything imaginable to no avail and suddenly solve the problem, the feeling of satisfaction is amazing."

"But how did you make a career out of it?" Martin asked.

"Several friends were always begging me to solve their computer problems, and most of them required an immediate solution, because they needed the computers for school or their jobs. I always felt bad when I had to put them off, because of the demands of my full-time job. When their friends and the friends of their friends also began showing up, I did some calculations ... or should I say wrote a program?" He smiled.

"Then I created a business plan, and decided I could make it my career. I wasn't setting the world on fire, but until recently the income was more than adequate."

"Until recently?" Pete asked. "What does that mean?"

"Some family issues, but I probably should just let it go at that."

Pete did, for the time being. Then, already knowing the answer, thanks to Alex, he asked, "Where is your business located?"

"I have a store in Highland Park. That's ideal for me, due to the location of my home. I can walk out the door and be at my store in minutes."

"Your business was located there when you filed the claim with Fundamentals Insurance?" Martin asked.

Daniel sighed and said, "Afraid so."

"Why do you say that?" Martin asked.

"Sorry, that was probably misleading." Daniel jutted his jaw out and scratched it. "My problem was with the handling of the insurance claim, not the location of my store."

"What problems did you have with the handling of your claim?" Martin asked.

"It was a long, drawn out, and painful process. For that reason, I'd never recommend Fundamentals Insurance to anyone," he said, running his fingers through his hair.

"In other words, the fault lies with the company, not the claims adjuster?" Martin asked.

"I don't know enough about the business to say, but I do blame the company for not keeping a tighter rein on Frederick Brooten."

"Tell us about your experiences with Brooten and the processing of your claim," Pete said.

A dark cloud passed over Daniel's face, he clenched his fists, stared through Pete and Martin, and began, "There was an electrical fire in the building that housed my business, or at least that was the cause, according to the fire marshal. Little was left of the building, and the contents not destroyed by the fire were destroyed by the water used to put it out. I was so thankful I had insurance. But the relief didn't last long. Everything was such a hassle, and it took more than six months for Fundamentals Insurance to process the claim."

"And Frederick Brooten was the claims adjuster?" Martin asked.

Daniel nodded forlornly. "The thing is, I needed that money to get my business up and running again. I had savings and investments, but they were being eaten up by other commitments."

Alimony? Child support? Both Pete and Martin had the same thought, but didn't ask, at least for now.

Kimball sighed and bit his lip. When it seemed he had nothing more to say, he continued, "Brooten was impossible. He coerced and threatened me. He forced me to sign a false claim, despite my protests, saying if I didn't go along with him, the entire claim would be rejected.

"I couldn't afford to have that happen. I had a lot of money tied up in that business, and he'd already dragged his feet with finalizing the claim. I was desperate. Even so, I called Fundamentals and asked to speak with the head of the small business division. They connected me with a man named Joseph Hardwick.

"Hard as I tried, I got nowhere with him. He said he'd spoken with others who'd attempted to get a larger settlement by disparaging their adjuster. He insisted that if there was a problem, it was with me, not with Frederick Brooten.

"After spending hours, trying to think of a way around Brooten, the best I came up with was going over Hardwick's head. So I called back and asked to speak with his supervisor. Can't tell you how defeated I felt when Hardwick again answered the phone. I threw up my hands in despair and signed the claim Brooten forced on me."

Suddenly, they were on some mighty thin ice, and Pete wasn't a gambler. So he stopped Kimball and Mirandized him, hoping if he had something to confess, this wouldn't cause him to change his mind. An encouraging sign was when Kimball didn't insist on an attorney, and he didn't demand they take him home.

Martin resumed the interview, asking, "You said Brooten coerced you? How did he do that?"

"First, like I said, he pressured me to file a false claim. It escalated the value of my losses and covered a couple of things it shouldn't have. We split the extra $40,000 down the middle. I felt guilty, but managed to rationalize it by telling myself it was going to a good cause. You see, I've been helping my grandfather, so I had a need ... an excellent use ... for the money. Just as important, if I didn't go along with him, like I said, he wouldn't submit the claim, and I'd get nothing. I didn't have the money needed to start over from scratch, so I'd have to abandon my business and find a new career. Easier said than done, and it meant I was a failure.

"One year later, almost to the day, Brooten came into the store and said I owed him another $5,000. I told him I didn't have it. I wasn't lying. He told me I had a week to find it, or else.

"I threatened to go to the top management of his company, and he laughed in my face. He said they were in on it, and that was why he needed more money. Based on my dealings with Hardwick, that seemed all too likely. So I told him I'd report Fundamentals Insurance to the Better Business Bureau, and he said if I did he'd bankrupt me. When I told him, 'Good luck,' he said I was oblivious to the possibilities, and he'd be happy to give me a demonstration. He had a comeback for every threat I thought of."

He took a sip of his drink and said, "Well, I'd already attempted to deal with others at Fundamentals Insurance. I thought about attacking it from another angle by writing a letter to the CEO, but didn't. The chances are zero to none that the CEO actually reads those letters, and if they saw it, they'd probably just speak to Brooten's supervisor. What good would that do? Also, I was in a time crunch and unable to wait who knows how long for nothing to happen?

"I did some research and discovered the only way to contact the Better Business Bureau was via email or snail mail. I did both, explaining the problems I was having. As best I can tell, they do nothing until they have enough complaints against a company ... however many that is. I have yet to hear back from them. I know I could have hired an attorney, but where was I going to get the money?

"A week later, Brooten returned. I told him I'd tried but couldn't get my hands on $5,000. He said I had one more week, and if I didn't have the money by then, I'd wish I'd never been born. I didn't know what he could do to me. I was afraid to find out. So I went to my bank and borrowed the money at an exorbitant interest rate. Of course he showed up, just like he said he would, and I gave him the money. By the way, it always had to be cash. He did the same thing on the two-year anniversary. Then a month ago, just three months after the two-year anniversary, he showed up again. When I saw him, I was sure he wanted more money. I was right. He demanded another $5,000." Kimball sighed and dragged a sleeve across his forehead, absorbing the sweat. His hand was shaking.

"Money is tight these days. My paternal grandmother died three years ago, and my grandpa wasn't making it on his own. He was lonely, not eating, and not caring for himself. Unfortunately, he doesn't have long-term-care insurance. My parents don't have room for him at their place, and I honestly don't think it would work out anyway. I'm not home enough to care for him, so the only option was assisted living. The good news is, he loves the place I found for him. He takes part in all kinds of activities, and he's thriving. The bad news is, these days those places cost a small fortune. I was managing to limp along, until Brooten got greedy." Kimball shook his head.

He looks like he's just lost his last friend, Pete thought.

"Worse yet," Kimball went on, "I knew it wouldn't end there. He'd keep coming back for more and, it seemed, at shorter and shorter intervals. I was kicking myself for ever insuring with his company, but a lot of good that was doing me.

"It looked like Brooten would ultimately cost me more than I got in the settlement. The stress was overwhelming, and I couldn't sleep at night. All I did was lie in bed, worrying and wondering what I could do."

There but for the grace of God ..., Martin thought.

"You think I did it, don't you," Daniel said. "And that's why you asked me to come here and answer a few questions, isn't it?"

"No, we didn't," Pete said. "All we knew is that you'd worked with Frederick Brooten on an insurance claim." That was true, and Pete feared what would happen to Daniel Kimball if one more person used him and put him through the ringer.

"How long have you known Bernice?" Martin asked.

"What difference does that make? She's been a blessing, listening to me, and understanding what Brooten put me through. I'll never be able to thank her enough. She's a saint."

Pete doubted their relationship started on a good note but, based on that speech, he didn't believe for a second he'd get Daniel to say anything negative about Bernice ... or tell the truth about their meeting. So instead he asked about other family members. He'd mentioned his parents, but not siblings, a wife, or kids.

"Just a sister in Ireland," he said. "She fell madly in love with an Irishman and now has dual citizenship. They have more kids than money, so I can't ask her to help with Grandpa, and I don't think I'll ever save enough to go see them. It breaks my heart." He sighed again and scratched his cheek.

"What kind of car do you drive?" Martin asked.

"A decrepit, beige Taurus. I'm worried how long I can make it last."

In other words, Pete thought, *he's willing to share a motive but obviously not confessing. Did he do it? We need to attack this from a new angle.*

So Pete came right out and asked, "How did you know when Brooten left for work and the route he followed?"

"I got his address off the internet, and he always bragged about starting work at 5:30, like that made him some kind of prized employee." Kimball rolled his eyes. "Anyway, I parked outside his apartment a few days, until I was able to follow him and determine his route to work."

"And?" Pete asked.

"Then I had to find the best place to lie in wait. But my choice would not have been the one selected by the person who did me a favor by killing him." Kimball took a breath and shook his head. "It could have been me, but it wasn't, and I think the person who did it should go free. Brooten was a blight on society, and I'm confident that every day he spent on this earth, he found a way to torture at least one person. No doubt my story is just one of dozens ... or even hundreds."

Martin asked, "Did you run into the person who did you that favor, while working on the details for your plan of attack?"

"Sorry, but you couldn't be more wrong if you think I'd say or do anything to hurt the person who was a lifesaver for me."

"Especially if that person qualifies as a saint in your book?" Pete asked.

Kimball responded with eyebrows raised and a hands-up shrug.

FORTY-TWO
The Gospel According to Bernice

Neither investigator relished the thought of dealing with their next interviewee, Bernice Bethel.

Before joining Pete and Bernice in Interview Room 2, Martin escorted Daniel past Pete's office and into the public area of HQ.

"I'll wait here for Bernice," he said.

"Sure," Martin said.

As soon as Martin arrived, Pete asked Bernice about her dealings with Fred Brooten.

"As far as Brooten was concerned, I was merely another of the nameless people who lived at the condominium complex over which he reigned. Neither my identity nor my needs and concerns were a consideration. The only thing that mattered to him were his preferences, desires, and power.

"Isn't a woman's home supposed to be her castle? For more than a year, I've felt like an unwelcomed intruder in Brooten's castle.

"In the two years he's been the president of our association, I spoke with him just once. That was more than a year ago, when I tried to explain we needed to make choices and operate within the limits posed by a realistic budget. I said that the rate at which the monthly dues were increasing would soon mean I could no longer afford to live there. He laughed and told me to put up or shut up.

"I somehow managed to stay calm and, hoping to get through to him, I told him that some of his actions exceeded the authority of the association's president and were in violation of the governing documents. He moved in close, too close for comfort, glared down at me, and told me no one cared what I thought.

"I tried to get enough people to attend the next annual meeting to reach a quorum and strip him of his authority. Can't even tell you the hours I spent going from door to door, attempting to protect my investment and maintain my residence in the condo I used to love and that has been my home for going on twenty years. I failed." She shook her head forlornly.

"After a lifetime of working hard, saving, and stretching every penny, I was on my way to a forced relocation. In and of itself, that would have been bad enough, but I honestly didn't know how I was going to garner the energy to find a new home, then pack up everything and move."

Pete nodded and said, "I understand you're the expert in your condominium complex when it comes to the arrivals and departures of not only your neighbors but also UPS, FedEx, and Amazon. Your neighbors refer to you as 'the all-seeing, all-knowing Bernice,' don't they?"

"So?"

"So you knew what time Fred Brooten left for work in the morning, didn't you?" Martin asked.

Staring at her hands, she nodded and said, "Yes."

"How did you know the route he took to work?" Pete asked.

"I followed him ... twice."

Before going any further, Martin Mirandized her, all the while wondering if it meant the end of her cooperation.

When she didn't request an attorney, Martin said, "Following him for two days makes it sound premeditated."

"Shooting out his tire was," she said, looking him straight in the eye.

"Explain," Martin instructed.

Bernice clenched her fists and said, "After I could no longer cope with the stress and the sleepless nights, I decided to do something that would make me feel better about a situation over which I had no control. So, like I just told you, I followed him to determine his route to work."

After a long pause, Pete said, "Go on."

"I arrived way too early. Didn't want to chance missing him." Bernice shuddered and continued, "As I'm sure you know, I'd picked the wrong day, thanks to the wind chill. Thought I was going to freeze to death while waiting for him. Found some consolation in knowing that too would solve my problem."

She paused again before adding, "I hid behind the undergrowth at the entrance to the Troutbrook Nature Sanctuary, waiting for him. I spent the whole time stomping my feet and moving my arms, fingers, and toes to avoid frostbite." She shivered.

"When he came over the hill on Jackson that's just north of Maryland Avenue, I took aim and shot out his front, driver's side tire. I did this while he was far enough away for me to have a more stable target, namely the front of the tire—the tread.

"He was hurting me, and I wanted to hurt him. That truck was the only thing I knew of that he cared about. He was fanatical about it. He got it washed every time it had a speck of salt or dirt on it. My plan was to force him to stop, hopefully be late for work, and be forced to deal with damage to that stupid truck."

"What happened next?" Pete asked.

Bernice pulled a tissue from a pocket and dried her forehead. Her hand was shaking. "As soon as the tire blew," she said, "he stopped, jumped out of the car, and stared at it. By the time he turned around, I was standing in the entrance to the Troutbrook parking lot. I wanted him to know who did it, even if it meant I had to buy a new tire. I wanted the satisfaction of having him know it was me, someone he'd belittled, made fun of, disregarded. And, well, I succeeded. He blew up and screamed, 'How dare you attack my baby! I'm going to kill you, you stupid bitch!'"

Bernice looked up, "I know people often say they are going to kill someone, but don't mean it literally. If you had seen the look in his eyes, you'd have known he meant it literally. With a look of sheer hatred, he came running at me with his arms and hands extended, like he planned to grab me by the throat and choke the life out of me. I expected him to be angry. I didn't expect anything like that. I'd parked my car about a block away on Old Maryland. He was coming for me, and the path he took blocked the route to my car. I panicked, wondering if I could escape. I began backpedaling, hoping to put enough distance between us to jut around his right side. I knew I could outrun him, but only if there was enough distance between us for me to get beyond his reach.

"Well, instead of achieving that, I stumbled and fell backwards as he lunged at me. I don't know exactly how it happened, but as I fell backwards or hit the ground on my butt, the gun fired, or went off, or whatever you call it. I had no idea where the bullet went."

"As soon as I hit the ground, I began rolling away, trying to keep him from landing on top of me and crushing me. I was panic stricken. My adrenaline was pumping. I thought I was going to die.

"The look of hate that had covered his face evaporated, and he came crashing down, landing on his belly with his arms still outstretched. That was the first time it occurred to me that the bullet might have struck him!" She looked up again.

"It must have taken a second or less for him to crash to the ground. By then, everything was operating in slow motion. He'd have landed on top of me, but by some miracle I'd rolled far enough away that he missed me by maybe a foot. I stared at him as I continued scrambling away. After he landed hard, and I mean really hard, because we're talking a lot of pounds dropping about three feet, I kept an eye on him as I escaped. I know I should have checked to see if he was still alive, but I was afraid to get within the reach of those long arms or the distance from which he could lunge at and reach me.

"He didn't move or make a sound. So I ran to my car and drove home, wishing the whole time I had my cellphone and could call 911. Did I have any idea he'd react so violently? Not a chance. Did I kick myself all the way home? You bet!" She sighed and shook her head.

Pete asked, "Wouldn't it have been far easier to slash or shoot out one of his tires in your condo parking lot, or did he always park in his garage?"

"I'd have preferred that for sure, and he never parked in the garage. Unfortunately, thanks to him, we have security cameras covering all the front doors and the entire parking lot. So that wasn't an option."

"What time did you arrive home?" Martin asked.

"Drove into my garage at 5:40 and walked in the door at 5:42."

Martin asked, "Did you call 911 then?"

"No. I was certain someone would have come across him before then. Hope I was right about that. Much as I hated him, I didn't want him to lie there suffering." She shook her head and blew out a long, slow breath.

"You're right. By then, someone had called 911," Martin said.

Bernice's shoulders relaxed a few degrees.

"What were you driving?" Pete asked.

"My car, of course."

"What kind of car do you have?" Pete asked.

"A 2004 Volkswagen Jetta."

"Color?" Pete asked.

"Silver."

"Best estimate, what time did you shoot him?" Martin asked.

"It had to be 5:25 or shortly after that. When I left home, I had no intention of killing him, and I wouldn't have gone had I been smart enough to foresee that it would end this way." She grimaced and rubbed the back of her neck.

"What kind of gun did you use?" Pete asked.

"A 9 mm Springfield Armory Hellcat."

"Where did you get it?"

"For a while, way back when, I dated a deputy sheriff from Rice County. He bought it for me, because he thought I needed a way to protect myself from, as he put it, 'all the crazies who live in the greater metropolitan area.'"

"Is it registered?" Martin asked.

"He never said."

Martin continued, "Do you have a permit to carry it?"

"I doubt it. I doubt he thought it would ever leave the confines of my home. Nor did I, until a few days ago."

"Where did you learn how to shoot?"

"He taught me. We used to go target shooting, and he kept at it until he was satisfied with my ability to hit the target with enough accuracy to defend myself."

"Where is the Hellcat now?" Martin asked.

"I'm not sure about the strength of the current. It's either on the floor of the Mississippi or on it's way to the Gulf of Mexico."

"And from what location was it launched?" Martin asked.

"Harriet Island."

"Who sent it on its way?" Martin asked.

With her head hanging low, Bernice raised her hand.

Pete asked, "How did you and Daniel Kimball get together?"

"For several days, I'd seen this car arrive in the condo parking lot around 5:00 a.m. The driver, a man, just sat inside until Brooten drove away. Couldn't help but wonder if he too had issues with Brooten that had escalated to the point of revenge. On the chance that was true, one day I wrote down the plate number. After

I shot Brooten, I was a basket case. I needed to talk to someone, but who? I couldn't talk to any of my neighbors."

She continued, "Out of desperation, in case I was right about his reason for hanging around our parking lot, I got the name and address for that plate. Then I went online and found a phone number. You see, if I was right about his reason for being there, who would understand better than him?" She smiled weakly.

"Danny didn't jump at the chance, but I finally succeeded in getting him to talk to and, even more important, listen to me. I was pretty messed up, and he helped me get my emotions under control. That was so kind and beneficial ... regardless of what happens to me."

"Why didn't you turn yourself in?" Pete asked.

'You didn't give me much time. It just so happens, we were discussing how to go about doing that when you arrived."

Pete left Bernice to Martin, went to his office, and contacted the on-call Ramsey County Attorney. She said she could reach headquarters in about thirty minutes. So he took Danny to Interview Room 2, and they placed an order with a downtown restaurant that delivered.

The assistant county attorney, Diane, arrived before the food, and Pete took her to his office, while Martin waited at the HQ entrance for the food.

Martin joined them as the assistant county attorney sat, eyes fixed on the screen, watching Bernice's confession for the second time. She peered at the screen, focusing on Bernice, her facial expressions and her body language.

Reaching the end, she looked at Pete and said, "You said he was 6'2" and pushing 300 pounds?"

Pete nodded and said, "And the woman is seventy-nine-years-old, seven or eight inches shorter, and a good 180 pounds lighter."

"Do you buy her story?" she asked him.

"Yes. I believe her when she said she tripped, causing her gun to discharge. It would be hard to find another explanation for the trajectory of the bullet that went through his neck, severing his brain stem, and killing him instantly." Pete continued his train of thought, "She said he was lunging at her as she tripped and landed on her backside. The positioning of his body when found by both a doctor who came upon the scene and the ME support that contention."

"If he wasn't intent on hurting her, why did he lunge at her? And what other explanation is there for the way he was outstretched with arms and hands extended when he died, and when he hit the ground? The fact that he died instantly explains the fact that he didn't reach for his neck. He was dead by the time the pain would have registered." You might contend that he tripped too. Have you ever tripped and tried to catch yourself by fully extending your arms out, shoulder height, rather than putting them at your side or sides or chest high?" Pete paused.

"Had he come down on her, there is little doubt that would have killed her."

Turning to Martin, Diane asked, "How about you?"

"I agree with Pete, and I think he's covered the bases."

Considering the facts, she said, "I understand and don't disagree with what you're saying, but this will be a political hot potato. It's unlikely we'd charge her with anything more than manslaughter for his death and/or criminal damage to property. I'll discuss it with the county attorney and get back to you on Monday. Do either of you believe she's a flight risk or a threat to society?"

"No," Pete and Martin said simultaneously, and Pete added, "I accessed Minnesota's Criminal History System and the nationwide criminal justice data systems. She has no record of arrests, or convictions for anything all the way down to a misdemeanor. We'll assure her we'll find her if she takes off. I'm confident she won't regardless. She wants to get this resolved."

FORTY-THREE
Love You More

The two investigators felt elated about solving this case so quickly, Pete's first since his return from paternity leave. They anxiously awaited the county attorney's decisions.

Pete felt pumped as well as drained. The long day had been packed with interviews and revelations. Some were more than a little surprising. Many were repeated recitations of the same facts. Knowing people like Brooten were thriving out there at the expense of a lot of good people was depressing ... and drove him to want to find ways to locate and disarm such piranhas.

He and Martin had managed only a can of Diet Coke for dinner. Nonetheless, all Pete wanted was to get home to Katie and Teddy. Martin seconded the motion to head home.

"Good work, partner," Pete said on their way out of headquarters. "See you Monday morning, barring the unlikely development that we're assigned another case before then."

"Yeah. Congratulations! Relax, and have a good weekend."

It was a few minutes past 10:00. Wearing a broad smile, Pete called Katie to let her know he was on the way. When she answered, he said, "We wrapped it up, aside from the paperwork. So I should have the weekend off. I'd love to spend it doing whatever you'd like."

Katie teased, "Does that mean I have to cancel my shopping trip, facial, and manicure? You're amazing, Pete. It'll be wonderful having you home this weekend."

"Yeah. I'll see you in about twenty minutes. Love you, Katie."

"I know. I love you more."

Teddy was asleep when Pete walked in the door and, as much as he'd have loved to hold him at that moment, he loved having Katie's arms around him. They sat that way for a long time, while he shared the details he was able to and stroked Benji.

Before getting ready for bed, Pete spent a few minutes looking down on Teddy, savoring a feeling of completeness. Just as he and Katie climbed into bed, Teddy awoke and was hungry.

Pete watched Katie nurse him, marveling at the connections between the three of them. He and Katie then played with Teddy for a while, before Pete resumed his role as chief rocker and singer to his son.

He loved the bond and relished the feel of Teddy's heartbeat as he held him close to his chest.

I'm so blessed, he thought. *What did I ever do to deserve this family? ... But what did any of the people we interviewed do to deserve Frederick Brooten?*

ACKNOWLEDGMENTS

My thanks to Pam McCord, Christopher Smith, Valerie Olson, Kris Olson, Jen Smith, Ethan Smith, Ellie Smith, and Brian McCord for their research assistance.

I'm also grateful to Ruth Krueger, Deb Harper, and Marly Cornell for sharing their proofreading and editorial expertise; and Christopher Smith for sharing his time and computer expertise.

Other books by S.L. Smith

Blinded by the Sight
Running Scared
Murder on a Stick
Mistletoe and Murder
Murder on Cathedral Hill
Last Breath
Dead Reckoning
A Party to Murder
The Trigger